Kisssssss

T0288151

Kisssss

a miscellany

STEVE KATZ

FC2

TUSCALOOSA

The University of Alabama Press
Tuscaloosa, Alabama 35487-0380

Copyright 2007 by Steve Katz
All rights reserved
First Edition

Published by FC2, an imprint of the University of Alabama Press, with
support provided by Florida State University and the Publications Unit of
the Department of English at Illinois State University

Address all editorial inquiries to: Fiction Collective Two, Florida State
University, c/o English Department, Tallahassee, FL 32306-1580

⊗

The paper on which this book is printed meets the minimum requirements
of American National Standard for Information Sciences—Permanence
of Paper for Printed Library Materials, ANSI Z39.48–1984

Library of Congress Cataloging-in-Publication Data
Katz, Steve, 1935-
    Kissssss : a miscellany / by Steve Katz.—1st ed.
        p. cm.
    ISBN-13 978-1-57366-139-3 (pbk. : alk. paper)
    ISBN-10 1-57366-139-2
    I. Title.
    PS3561.A774K57 2007
    813'.54—dc22
                                            2007012344

Cover Design: Lou Robinson
Book Design: Joe Amadon and Tara Reeser
Typeface: Baskerville
Produced and printed in the United States of America

CONTENTS

CURRENT EVENTS

The light was red. At the bottom of the hill an '71 Fairlane pulled up next to a Honda Civic. Rick, the kid driving the Fairlane, and his friend, Nolly, riding shotgun, both looked to their right at the driver of the Civic. It was Eighth Street, so it was one-way. Rick pointed at the dude, who had long blonde hair slicked back, narrow wire-rimmed glasses, and a black baseball cap worn backwards. "Pink that one."

"About time," said Timarie, one of the girls in the back seat. "Something." She pressed the Indiglo button on her watch. "If you hurry we can still make the movie."

"I'm like raging so much in here," said Willie, the other girl. "I want to see Sharon Stone do what's-his-name. Or maybe it was vice versa. Candy said it. I don't care." She leaned over the front seat and looked at Rick, "I just need to see it..."

"You mean Richard Gere?"

"No. I don't think so."

"Alec Baldwin? Tom Hanks?"

"No. Not that..."

"Michael Keaton? John Travolta."

"Don't be stupid, and it's not even Woody Allen, either. And Denzel Washington, not."

Everyone laughed.

Nolly rolled down the shotgun window and signaled the dude in the Honda, as if to ask directions. The dude rolled his window down.

"Hurry up, Snakefoot, the light's gonna change," said Rick.

"So how do you get to Wall Street from here, mister man?" said Nolly as he lifted his Glock and squeezed off three into the dude's face.

"Don't call me Snakefoot again," he said as they turned the corner and drove east. "My name is Nolly."

"What kind of a name is Nolly?"

"Who would want to steal an '71 Fairlane?" asked Harriet, as she looked at every car in the parking lot of the Roxxy Art Theater.

Gloria shrugged. "People don't even know what they're stealing any more. It's a different world."

"I should call the police, I guess. I never had my car stolen before. I hate to go through all that. Police and questions and forms to fill out."

"I don't mind talking to the police," said Gloria. "I'll call them for you." In fact, Gloria liked talking to the police. She watched a lot of television. Reruns of *Hill Street Blues*, especially, and *NYPD Blue*, and *Law & Order*, her faves. Talking to the police made her feel like she was practically on television. She almost wished it had been her own car stolen, except she didn't own a car.

Harriet leaned against the corner of the theater building with her pinky in her nose, and stared blankly into the parking lot. They had just seen *Farewell My Concubine*, an epic movie, like an old Cecil B. DeMille spectacular. China had swept her away in the movie, even though the brutal training of the young boys in the first part had made her very uncomfortable. She definitely wanted to go to China, maybe even learn a little conversational Chinese first. In the parking lot she could see a BMW, a new Mazda, a Lexus, an Infiniti, a Cadillac, Volvos. Why did they pick on her ancient Fairlane? It would make her sad to lose that car. It was the last of her connection with her ex-husband's family. He had signed the car over to her a year before the divorce. The divorce was bitter, and had blindsided her, because neither herself nor any of her friends would have expected Gil to dump her in that way, just not show up one night for dinner, and before she knew it, before she even took his peejays off his pillow, he's living with a young kid, a boy, downtown in a loft in Lodo. It was a month before he even left a message. She never even got his address 'til a year later. She never suspected he had these tendencies. He was so moralistic in general, so judgmental about other people's lives. Her AIDS test at least was negative, thank God. He said specifically that she could keep the car, even though it was already in her name. It was the car his grandmother had given him. Blow it up, was what she thought at first, shoot him down with his little fairy friend outside their apartment. But she didn't. It had only 57,000 miles on it, a real old lady's car. She felt at home in it.

"It's going to take them at least an hour to get here," Gloria said when she came back. "It's so warm. Oodles of crime everywhere."

Harriet suddenly was laughing, and Gloria put a hand on her shoulder to comfort her, taking the laughter for a case of nerves. In fact, Harriet was shaking a little from the stress of the theft and the memories. "Everything's gonna work out," Gloria told her.

"I lost my virginity in that car was what I was thinking. Gil fucked me my first time in the passenger seat. I got him to do it; I mean, of course I wanted to lose that. I liked the idea of losing it in Grandma's brand new car. Of course Gil was really

11

fussy. He didn't want to get it dirty. He put down his sweater, and his shirt under my butt, first; and there I went. So I always had the idea that my virginity was still in the car, and now it's been stolen, my virginity lost and then stolen. I think whoever stole it will have some bad luck."

"I liked it and I didn't like it," said Michael.

This was the first time he and Sarah had gone to a movie together. They had started dating three weeks before, when Reggie introduced them in the computer class. Reggie was the handsome nerd who taught the class. He couldn't have been more than twenty-two himself, recently graduated, still wearing his baseball cap backwards. Reggie was unnerved by the obvious attraction Sarah, who must have been in her thirties, was showing him, licking her lips when he leaned over her station to explain macros. You could taste the relief the young man felt when he introduced Sarah to Michael, and saw some interest boot up. He turned away to leave them to test their compatibility. So it was out of a sense of retreat, second best, that Sarah agreed to go out with Michael, an acknowledgement that she could no longer easily offer herself where she willed as a flower to be plucked.

Both of them had just come off difficult separations. Michael's last squeeze terminated when his former, Susan, took a Peace Corps contract to work as a nurse in Sri Lanka. He suspected she'd signed the contract in order to get away from him, not a difficult conclusion. Michael knew he had been an oppressive bastard with her, dominating her life while she went through nursing school. He had ten years on her when they first got together, she being only seventeen at the time. He was willing to be the father she never had, and at a certain point after she got out of nurse's training, even he realized, *basta*—she had had enough—but he didn't know how to back off. For that reason he had resolved with Sarah not to seem too opinionated or overbearing.

For her part, Sarah had dumped Otis on a bet with her girlfriend, Nicole, who dared her to do it. Codependent was the catchword, Nicole saying she was afraid to give up the comfort of his sponging off her. It was a relief finally to be done with it, and as a payoff Nicole had taken her to a Michael Bolton concert, who she thought was like Fabio with emotions and a voice. For both of them, Bolton was the ideal man: strong, emotional, though they didn't know that much about him, except that he had daughters, and that he really cared about them, lucky girls.

Neither Michael nor Sarah knew if they wanted to be in a relationship again, and that gave them what they felt was a certain amount of freedom to be loose with each other. He certainly didn't want a young woman again, delicious as youth could appear. Sarah, too, was being cautious. She surely didn't want another Otis in her life. She knew that attraction and pain were toggled on the same switch. That was why her response to Michael's comment about the movie was inadvertently hostile.

"Isn't that kind of wishy-washy, liked it and didn't like it?"

Sweat pressed out at his temples. He wasn't used to being taken to task like that for something he said. Susan certainly never did it, though they might have been happier at the end if she had. In this situation he was trying to be careful and correct.

"What I meant by that was…"

13

"Oh my God," her hand flew up to cover his mouth. "I can't believe this. Look, Otis—"

She couldn't believe she'd called him Otis. She so embarrassed herself; but he didn't know her former's name, so she let the mistake slide. "Look, Michael."

As he saw her looking over his shoulder with her dark eyes widened that way and her lips drawn back, Michael was reminded that when he had first seen her in the computer class he had remarked to himself that she looked like a rat; and with her long professionally whitened incisors glinting in the coffeehouse track lighting she looked even more rodentine.

"Look! Look!" she insisted.

Michael thought it could be a trick—when he turned she'd make his Napoleon disappear—but he turned anyway. "Gosh," he said, spontaneously. Rarely in his life had he ever said "gosh." The two actors from *Farewell My Concubine* had just walked through the door. They were dressed in mostly western clothes, though they were made up as if to perform the play within the movie, one of them with a kimono over his jeans. It was like *The Rocky Horror Picture Show* in vice versa.

When she spotted the actors entering the coffeehouse Gloria gasped, blowing the foam of her cappuccino across the table. Harriet was indisposed in the bathroom, and Gloria was keeping an eye on the door, in case the police arrived. They had arranged to meet them at the coffeehouse. A quick look around the crowded room made Gloria realize the actors would probably sit down at the table right in back of theirs. "Oh my god," she thought. She really didn't know what to think. If it had been Mel Gibson or Richard Gere, perhaps she could have thought more clearly.

By the time Harriet returned, the actors were settled at their table, energetically conversing, oblivious to the rest of the room.

"Do you remember their names? That pretty one is Dee, something like that."

"Whose names?"

"Turn around and look at that table, but don't make it too obvious. The one drinking the giant mocha, I mean. The pretty one."

Harriet turned, then turned back quickly. "Oh my God, they're right next to us. How did they get here?"

"Maybe they knew we were here," Gloria said. They both giggled into their cups. "I think his name was Dede, or something. God, we just saw the movie. And the big one is Louie, I think. The one with the iced tea."

"Do you think they're the real actors? Why would they come here?"

"I wish I could understand what they are saying."

"I don't have time. I have to look out for the cops when they come. Some day I'll learn Chinese."

Gloria leaned their way to try to recognize the voices, and she realized she understood what they were saying. It was English. They were speaking the subtitles.

"*I've eaten my candied crab apples. I'm a fucking star already,*" said the pretty one with the stripe of mocha along his upper lip. Gloria wasn't sure that was his line in the film.

"*What does it take to become a star,*" said the big one with the iced tea. "*How many beatings?*"

"They're talking English," Gloria leaned back to tell Harriet, who was staring hard at the door, as if only her concentration could get the cops to arrive.

"I'm so strong I can uproot mountains," sang the pretty one, rising slightly from his seat with the line.

"Sorry this took so long," said the waitperson with a circle of blue ivy tatted around her bicep. She set a plate in front of Harriet.

"I didn't order anything," said Harriet. She leaned closer to the plate. "Not this. What is it?" It protruded from the center of the plate, bathed in what looked like a raspberry sauce, so she assumed it must be sweet.

The waitress had moved on to another table.

"Since the Chu king has lost his fighting spirit, why should his favorite concubine value his life?"

Gloria was dizzy, reliving this powerful movie over a cappuccino, like post-cinematic stress disorder. It wasn't comfortable.

Harriet grabbed her arm, "You know what this is?" Harriet pointed at the thing on the plate, her forefinger tipping the tip of it.

"No matter how resourceful you are you can't fight fate."

Gloria stared at the pinkish thing on Harriet's plate. "Of course I know."

"Tell me."

"It's a nose."

"Looks like it, doesn't it?"

"I recognize it."

"What do you mean, recognize?" Harriet flipped it onto its side with her long latte spoon. "How do you recognize it?"

"I'm almost sure. That's Harvey Keitel's nose."

"Not! How would you know?"

"We saw that movie a couple of weeks ago. He had tattoos on it."

"No! Not! Even if, how do you know it's Harvey Keitel's?"

"I go to lots of movies. I've seen all Harvey Keitel's movies. *Reservoir Dogs*. You saw that one with your eyes closed. And *GoodFellas*. It's an educated guess, but I know that nose. *Things of Desire*. Remember? That was Harvey Keitel who was formerly known as an angel.

"Why did they serve me this nose?" It made Harriet nervous. She would have left just then, except she had to wait for the police. "This is a coffeehouse. Nobody serves nose in this city."

"I've followed my king on his military campaigns, enduring wind, frost, and hard toil. I hate only the tyrant who plunged our people into a life of misery."

"Ask the waitress. Take it up there and ask them."

Harriet had enough on her mind already.

"My king, quickly give me your famous sword."

Harriet took the plate back to the counter. "I didn't order this," she said.

"I'm sorry," said the tattooed woman. She turned to her co-workers. "Didn't someone order this Bobbit thing, this special?"

"That was dope. Totally whack," said Timarie as they emerged into the lobby. "Especially where she flashed her pussy at him from her chair at the what-do-you-call-it, when they were questioning her. Did you see that?"

"No, man. I never notice the pussy. I missed it. I was busy licking ashtrays in the smoking," said Nolly, a hand on the 9-mm under his belt under his shirt.

"That embarrassed me," said Willie. "I couldn't have done that in front of one of those big cameras."

"You fucked in front of a camera. I was there."

"That was different. This was Sharon Stone, man. I was embarrassed for her. Anyway, I don't like that word, *pussy*. It don't sound right."

They walked out into the parking lot and looked around. There were tons of cars.

"I'm gonna buy that Wagoneer over there, man. Our Fairlane is way past its warranty by now," Rick said.

Willie was shaking her head. "Shit, I don't wanna ride in no Jeep. I was embarrassed in that fuckin' Fairlane. It was so old. There's all these other cars on the lot, man; like, even that red Camaro."

"Shut the fuck up."

"From now on," said Timarie, "I'm never gonna wear underpants. It gives a big advantage to a girl. And I'll wear a dress, so when it comes in handy to show your slit, there it is. It's whack, man."

"I didn't even see it. When did it happen?" Nolly grinned, and pinched Timarie's nipple.

"That's because you a faggot, man. Faggots can't see pussy."

"Slap it shut, bitch, or I will."

"Well you can't see mine, anyway. Not unless you pay me. And don't be cheap."

The Wagoneer swung around and stopped by the three of them. Timarie looked in. "I don't want to ride in there. They feed their dogs in there."

"Shut up and get in before the Boy Scouts get here."

"It stinks."

"Your breath, man. That's what stinks."

"You better buy nicer cars, man; or, I'm gonna start riding with Frankie. He asked me."

"Frank asked you? That's dope, man. You should ride with him," said Willie.

"I know it. He wouldn't buy the fuckin' Jeep, man." Timarie climbed into the shotgun seat, and looked down at Rick. "O, slap that chop back in your pants, man. Drive this funk."

"You suck him while we drive. I like it out in the fresh air. Then we park up the hill there by Wizenor's Park, and we do some nasty."

"Man, you don't know me yet. I study with Lorena, man. You put it back where it belongs, or I cut off that dick and give it back to you mama."

"I'll beat you across the knees with it, bitch. You'll never skate again."

"You'll miss the spot, just like them hopeless lames."

In the back of the Jeep Willie wore a baby seat on her head while Nolly tongued her nipples. The Jeep pulled out of the parking lot, drove a few blocks west, and started to climb a hill. There was no moon. The stars were out full blast.

Their poor Reggie was the victim. Neither Sarah nor Michael had ever been this close to a victim of the current plague of automatic weapon teenage drive-by violence. The newspapers were full of it. Public radio was full of it. TV was full of it, especially MTV, where gangsta rap and some of the hip-hop were full of it. Movies appeared, that were also full of it. But this was their first near experience of it. Of course, it hadn't happened directly to them, and they had known Reggie only as an instructor, but the news landed on them like a ton of unwelcome gigabytes. Reggie had, after all, been responsible for getting them together. Somehow, as tragedy often does, this made them feel closer to each other, in their mutual emotional cyber-slump, that was complicated by Sarah's choosing to work in MS because that system was in general use in her office, whereas Michael had chosen to work in Mac because he felt it could more quickly satisfy his urge to be creative. Following the lead of the other students, they taped ribbons of black crepe to their monitors. Many wept as they looked at their screens, and a message came up on both IBM and Mac that everyone was invited to contribute to a fund to defray costs of the funeral. Reggie had a family, but the mom and dad were persistent hippies living incommunicado in Southeast Asia. Michael turned to look at Sarah working in the row of IBMs against the opposite wall. She leaned forward to consult a manual and her sweater pulled out of the waist of her black stirrup pants to reveal a line of her tattoo on the chalk-white knife-edge of flesh. Michael turned back to his screen where he was trying not to wilt against the many complications of Adobe Photoshop. Just his luck, he thought, to finally meet a woman he liked, but was forced to separate from because she worked in DOS. Sarah had a similar conflict. She was learning to surf the Internet, and didn't know yet if it would be possible to communicate across the chasm that separates DOS from Mac. Along with her skepticism about relationships in general, she knew it could be an added strain if email created difficulties.

As soon as she fired up the Fairlane, the cops pulled away. It had taken a couple of days to find it. Whoever stole it had left the car in the farthest space of the northeast corner of the United Artists parking lot, almost in the woods. They hadn't damaged it any more than the few familiar dents she had been carrying on it. She let it idle as she adjusted the mirror. The cop car swung around, and for a few moments lit up her back seat, and she saw something there. Before going to the art theater to see *Farewell My Concubine* she had cleaned everything out. The dome light no longer worked, so she shined her Mini Maglite into the back seat. She was surprised they hadn't stolen it from her glovebox. She lit up some blankets, a plastic tote of baby stuff, and a scatter of clothing odds and ends. She reached over, and shifted the blankets. "Oh," she exclaimed, "a baby." The cops were already gone. They couldn't have been very thorough. A whole baby they had missed. It was asleep, looking peaceful and cute, but she knew that wouldn't last. Babies cry. They shit in their diapers. That's their job. That was why she had decided at a certain point never to have one herself. Tolerance and patience were not her virtues. She preferred maybe something that barked, though she never got one of those, either. All she'd ever had was Gil, and now he was gone, all but his car.

The baby started to twist its mouth into a terrifying suck-and-pucker. That was definitely something she preferred not to deal with. She hated to go back to the police, who had been so gruff with her, letting her know they had more important things to think about than her damned Fairlane. She wished Gloria was with her. Gloria liked babies.

As she slowly swung the car around some people ran into her headlight beam. They had popped out of the woods and were rushing towards her, waving their arms. Her first thought was to speed up and get out of there, but she noticed that one of the people was a little girl, and another a smallish woman. The man, gaunt and unshaven, with a pitiful expression of grief and urgency, not at all threatening, tapped on her window, and signaled for her to roll it down.

"Pliz. Pliz. Bebby. Car, home. Bosnia, Bosnia, Bosnia."
He slapped his chest as he said Bosnia.

"Is this your baby?"

"Pliz. Yes. Pliz. Bebby. Girl bebby." He pointed at the creature in the back seat about to start crying. "Sofia bebby. Wife, Halifa. Me, Muhamet. Live home car. Live car. Pliz."

"You were living in my car?" It happened fast, she thought.

"You're from Bosnia?"

"Bosnia. Bosnia. Bosnia." He banged his chest some more. "Many pipples dead. Dead pipples war."

"I'm very sorry. This is my car. It's a Fairlane. I have the keys."

He gasped as if he couldn't find enough air to say the words. The little girl came to the window, and he lifted her. She smiled, revealing some missing teeth. "Sleep car. Pliz. Bebby. Mine bebby sleep and mama. Bosnia war."

The baby started to cry. She couldn't stand it. Questions like: How did they get here from Bosnia? How can they live in a car? Where do they eat? crossed her mind; then they crossed her mind out.

"Take your baby." She unlocked the back door. The whole family jumped in and sat down.

"Car home," said the father. The baby had big lungs.

"No. Bosnia home."

The whole family together beat their chests. "Bosnia, Bosnia, Bosnia," they wailed in unison.

Harriet couldn't stand it. She got out of the car, and looked in at the family. "Okay," she shrugged.

"Okay, America," said the man.

"Okay," said the woman softly, as the baby slurped onto her breast.

In an instant, Harriet decided to leave it all behind. She headed for the bus stop, and abandoned everything—the car with the memory of Gil and his grandmother, and all the feeble ghosts of her virginity.

"Can't believe. No, man. What I just saw. I can't believe it, man."

Only Timarie was still awake. Willie snored in the back, and Rick's lips flapped against the steering wheel.

"You gotta come look with me. This is—" He grabbed her shoulder. "This you gotta see, Timarie."

"Yeah. Right. Rick wakes up and kills me if I'm gone with you."

"You gotta be quiet, though. But you gotta come."

Nolly pulled on her. She knew she had to go. She quietly opened the door, but something started beeping. "Fuckin' Jeep," she mumbled, and ripped out some wires under the dash so the beep stopped. She lowered Rick's head from the steering column to lay it across her seat. He shifted his body. He was out.

Timarie followed Nolly into the woods. It all felt to her like a different movie from the one they had seen. Through the trees they could see an edge of brightness pushing at the dark eastern sky. It was no longer late. It was early. Another day might come. He stopped, and held her back with his arm.

"Shhh!"

They could hear a faint clank of metal against metal.

"That's them," Nolly whispered.

"Who?"

"Shh. I don't know. Come."

They got low and crawled farther through the trees, where they saw the beams of flashlights whipping around the underbrush. Timarie was getting into this, like it was a real movie. Nolly had his gun jammed into his belt at his back. They crawled behind a rock at the edge of the cliff that overlooked the United Artists parking lot.

"Who are they?" asked Timarie.

"Fuck do I know?"

There was more light. They could see the men were white, which always made them suspicious. They were dressed in combat fatigues, which was worse. They had some guns set up pointing towards the parking lot. "Mortars," whispered Nolly. Bits of conversations carried toward them on the dawn breeze.

"That ain't Spanish, *vato*," said Timarie.

"What the fuck are they doing? Why are they here?"

Timarie looked down at the parking lot. "That's the car. Ain't that the Fairlane we just traded? Look, there's people around it. People are in it too." She looked back to the men with mortars. "This is like something you get on TV. Like some war. You gotta do something, Nolly."

Nolly pulled his gun from under his belt and looked at it. He checked the clip. Three rounds gone. He looked at Timarie. She saw fear in his face. "What can I do?"

The men in fatigues were lifting mortar rounds out of their crates.

"*Santa Maria y Jesu.* Do something quick. Those people down there are gonna get blown up if you don't do something."

"So, what? What can I do anyway?"

The first mortar round blew about eighty yards from the car. The soldiers adjusted quickly as the family scrambled below.

"There's kids there. There's women gonna die. Nolly. Do something. Give me the fuckin' gun."

Nolly handed her the 9mm and crawled back toward the Jeep. Timarie looked at the gun. She had never fired a gun. She pointed it at the men in fatigues. Several mortar rounds went off below, one followed by a big explosion as the car was hit. She squeezed the trigger. Nothing happened. She turned to ask Nolly how to shoot, but he was gone, so she looked at the gun again. *Sig Sauer* was engraved on the handle. That didn't mean anything to her. She squeezed again and nothing happened. Nolly had taken the clip with him. She stepped out toward the men, holding the gun in two hands like they did in the movies. "Stop," she said. "Just stop." The men in fatigues were startled to see her, and they stepped back from the mortars, then they started to laugh. *"Parar! Detener!"*

She didn't know if she was using the right word, but she was pissed. "Stop the guns. Don't kill those people." She squeezed the trigger again. The laughing stopped and she stood there. She stood there for about sixteen seconds.

After several days, Gloria returned to the coffeehouse alone. She half-expected the actors still to be there; after all, the movie was still running. It was late and there were no customers. They were ready to close. The tattooed waitress was obviously annoyed that she had come in. "To go," Gloria said immediately, to reassure her. The waitress became friendlier.

"What would you like?"

"I was in a couple of nights ago." She tapped her nose. "You had a thing." She didn't know how to say it.

"You mean the special?"

"Yeah. It was a special."

The waitress brought it in a take-out box, with the sauce on the side. "This is the last one." She handed back Gloria's money. "It's on us."

Gloria set the box on her bed and hung up her coat. She got into her peejays and straightened up the shrine and cushion where she meditated, then opened the Styrofoam take-out box. Without the sauce on it, this looked even more like Harvey Keitel's nose, tattooed, but without a septum. Maybe too much cocaine. She grinned. When she meditated she grinned a lot. But she could have been mistaken; maybe it wasn't Harvey Keitel's nose. She could call his agent and find out. No, she was sure it was; anyway, it made no difference. She had no inclination to bite into the nose. It was just a model, anyway, a simulacrum. But she did have a peculiar inclination to wear it over her clitoris while she sat. The word, *clitoris*, still made her uncomfortable, though she was grateful for it. Before her procedure was completed, the nub had been the tip of her penis, and it felt to her fingers very much like the tip of her former organ. She didn't know why, but felt it would be right to cap it with Harvey Keitel's nose.

No one in Denver, her new city, knew she had formerly been a guy, not even her best friend, Harriet. The children she had fathered were still living in Harrisburg, Pennsylvania, and hadn't yet come to see her. Maybe some day. She understood it was complicated for them. It was complicated for her; for instance, was she Grandpa, or was she Grandma? She dreaded running into her ex-Special Forces buddy, Mike Sugman, who she knew lived somewhere around Denver. At the same time there was a thrilling possibility, after all they had been through together, of becoming his girlfriend, or his mistress if he was married.

There were some things about being a woman she still needed to smooth out, although as a woman she felt she had definitely become more herself. Meditation helped, meditation on the body of woman. She used to pray, but she stopped doing that. When you prayed, you prayed for something concrete; for instance, he had prayed a lot for the body of a woman; but you meditate to empty your mind of all desire, to stop the painful attachment to thought and emotion. If she were ever to pray for something again, aside from asking for a man who would truly love her and care for her, it would be to be granted the function of menses. She knew she would penetrate further into her womanhood if she could only menstruate, at least once, just to know it, just to deepen her kinship with the moon. No one who had counseled Gloria had advised her what her womanhood might be after menopause, how sad it might be.

But this was all right. She felt really good about herself now. She didn't know if the impulse to cap her clitoris with this particular nose was sexual or what. Was it just crazy? Was it demeaning to herself as a woman? Did other women have such notions? She hadn't yet had time enough as a total woman to think this all through. She'd learned other things—to relax and let men open car doors for her, to let them slide restaurant chairs under her butt. But now she was alone, in the privacy of her own meditation corner. And when she was through, she decided, she would attach the nose to her small Corning cutting board with Krazy Glue, and then cover it with polyester resin to preserve it forever for herself.

She turned off the electric lights, lit a candle and a joss stick, and lowered her butt to the cushion, and sat still to gather herself for a moment before she slipped Harvey Keitel's nose over her clitoris. It fit like a cap, and that made her grin. This felt like some mischief, and she liked that. As she breathed she repeated the mantra that guru what's-her-face had given her during one expensive weekend at the ashram in the Catskills. The mantra was SO on the inbreath, HAM on the outbreath. SO HAM, SO HAM, SO HAM. It translated roughly as *I am that, I am that, I am that.*

THE INFORMATION HIGHWAY

The sexual act deflates the imagination.
People always seem stupider afterwards.

—*Malcolm de Chazal*

"Roger, sweetheart, please stop," Adeline complains. "I'm not your Snack-o-Matic." He's a passionate guy, with great feelings, the sweetest lover, but his face has been rooting between her thighs since one a.m. of Halloween. "I love it, but there's a limit, even to pleasure, Mighty Mouth. It's been twenty-four hours, no, twenty-two, no, twenty-seven hours by now. It's almost five." She went as a bag of golf clubs, and he as a marijuana plant; however, the big party they had anticipated turned out to be a sedate gathering of her corporate cronies dressed as company products. So they cut out and walked the streets for a while, taking in the human marshmallows and spareribs and shish kebabs. Barbecue was a big theme this year. They saw some superheroes, too; and wizards, and one couple dressed as the Twin Towers, and a whole sorority of witches that emptied out of the Lido bar and marched down Broadway. There must have been sixty of them.

"Stop, Roger. I love you bunches, but please now, stop." She doesn't want to hurt the feelings of this sensitive, caring, long-haired, gentle vegetarian guy, the one man she loves; but they have hardly slept. "Save some for a rainy day, Rog, honey. You know I'm happy to be where your next meal is coming

31

from, forever. I promise." Even in their ordinary life there is some truth in that. She's the one who brings home the brie. "I'm a whole person. You don't have to think of me all the time as some munchies." She feels her sense of humor slipping away.

Roger lifts his head to face her face. "Almost finished. It's the ABCs of it, even the XYZs of it," he intones. His face looks as if it has been dipped in a vat of lanolin, her stuff thick even in the eye sockets, and the whole prolate sphere textured here and there with her pubic curls. Can he see? She hopes not. She hates to look at it, so she sinks it back down.

It's five a.m. now, Sunday morning. Good thing she doesn't have to go in to work. She's hungry, but can't think of anything she really wants to eat. *Shoah* is on the all-night art film channel. She can't remember if she saw it years ago at the theater or not. It's engrossing, but very painful to watch, even in the throes of this pleasure. Full of stink, of lies and hypocrisy. Maybe that's why it comes on at four a.m.

At the commercial break she pulls on Roger's ponytail. Enough is enough. She's a woman who works for a living. "Sweetheart, come on," she entreats. To her astonishment the head starts to separate from the neck. She stops, but it won't fit back. It continues to separate with a pleasant, Velcro-like crackle. Velcro is one of the few benefits to the population at large that she can understand from the cost-inefficient space age. "Stop this, Roger," she says, and rolls the head back, pushing from the crown to refit it to the neck, but no luck. It is already half-detached. She looks around the room, as if afraid there might be a witness.

When they got home he said, as if he had learned about romance only from pornography, "I want to give you head all night." So this is what happens when words of lust take a literal turn. It won't screw, it won't chink back in. She will either have to leave it dangling, or take it off the rest of the way. She's famous for finishing whatever she starts, so dangling for her is not an option. There's a reason she has climbed the corporate ladder, has penetrated the glass ceiling. She knows it sounds ridiculous, but she says, "Okay, relax, sweety," and she gives the graying ponytail another tug. It comes off easily, just like ripping wet newsprint. Then she lies back and holds it above her face to look at this. "Gosh, pumpkin. What happened? I'm so sorry." The head is thickly coated with herself. The tongue, curled into a tube, sticks far out from the lips. One eye winks at her. A slight sneeze.

"Sweetheart, yuk!" Her revulsion reflex makes her toss the head at the bathroom door, where it rolls into the fresh kitty litter, one of her company's original products, picking up most of it on the face before it comes to rest near the sink, its features spackled with green, chlorophyl-impregnated chips.

"Roger is a novelist," says Adeline aloud, another irrelevant thought. The novel is something to read on a flight to Indianapolis, when you don't have work to do. She had shown Roger how to use the Mac in the first place, and that was a help to him. By itself the novelist is an anachronism. A novel can be written as well by committee or a computer can be programmed to produce it. She factored all this in when she chose to live with Roger. He presented a contrast to her professional life, put a quaint spin on her personal time.

She shakes the nightgown loose from where it's sticking to her thighs, and follows Roger's head into the bathroom. It rests on its side under the washstand. "Everything will be perfect, darling. I can handle everything." She drags the head across the floor to lean it face-out in the crotch the clothes-hamper makes with the bathtub, and secures it in place with a beach towel rolled up.

"Oh Roger, baby," she says, after gazing a few moments on the face. "If this has happened to you, what do you think God has in store for me?" The word *God*, from her own mouth, unnerves her. She uses that word only with her grandmother.

As soon as she steps back the eyes open and the lips move. The head starts talking. "Lift is produced by the difference in pressure between the upper and lower surfaces of the airfoil, or wing. Since the pressure of a gas is inversely proportional to its speed you shape the wing to maximize the speed of the air across the upper surface. The characteristic lifting airfoil profile has a maximum thickness of six to eighteen percent of the chord aft of the leading edge. The normal component, or lift, may be expressed in equation form as $L = C \text{ sub } l \text{ sub } q\, S$. The variation of C sub L with geometric angle of attack..."

She finds his voice more nasal than before, although she recognizes it as Roger; but she can't bear to listen, and decides to wash downstairs in the guest bathroom. Roger's body now stands on his own two feet in the bedroom. An erection has developed. "So that's what it takes," Adeline thinks, then thinks better. The right arm is extended and bent, pointing at the baby bazooka with a crooked forefinger. The body seems to follow this stiff thing around as it bumps into things, like someone in love. She's afraid at first to approach, but then finds it quite docile as she takes the left hand, leads it to the bed, and lowers it to the sheet. The penis seems to be pleading for someone to grab it. Not her, not now. With another sheet she covers this, so the thing stands like a tent-pole in the midst.

As she scrubs in the guest shower she maps her whole week. It will be Thursday before she has time to get back to this Roger situation, but it isn't so catastrophic to delay since everything is more or less alive. The ability to speak, the sustaining of erection, that was life enough for a man. She could wash the . head when her schedule permitted. The kitty litter is a stellar product. It would keep the thing fresh at least until Thursday.

She spends most of the day in her bathrobe in the office downstairs, editing the manual some of her writers produced for a new investment-tracking program. They made the new software seem too complicated. Better the other way around. Then she works on her laptop on a PowerPoint presentation she is going to make for her board. To avert a hostile takeover she has fashioned a sexy offering for their stockholders, and leveraged a distribution deal that will get their swift new RAM expanders into every computer store in the country. This is only one aspect of the diversification she has designed for a corporation that before herself languished in the business of pet products.

At 9:30 she's ready for bed. The morning disaster has almost slipped her mind, but approaching her bedroom she hears Roger's head still yacking in the bathroom.

"Partially balanced incomplete blocks form a very general class of experimental design in which not all treatments occur in every block. 1.) Each treatment is replicated r times. 2.) Given any treatment..."

Roger's poker has doubled in length. Business has doubled twice since she became CEO, she reflects. So she appreciates doubling. But Roger's thing could be like Jack's beanstalk. Who knows where it will end up? For the first time in the three years they've lived together she feels ambivalent about crawling into bed with Roger, even though the snoring problem is probably eliminated by this coup; but realistically, the longer erection has pulled the sheet into a higher tent now, and she will be at a definite disadvantage in what sometimes becomes a nasty battle for the comforter in the middle of the night. She intended to get a second one, but as with a lot of things domestic hasn't found time or motivation to shop for it. The major concerns of the day always distract her from the minor difficulties of the night.

She hears the head, still blabbing in the bathroom.

"After having been twice driven back by heavy, southwestern gales, Her Majesty's Ship *Beagle*, a ten-gun brig, under the command of Captain Fitzroy, sailed from Devonport on the 27th of December, 1831. The object of the expedition..."

Wrong! She can't tolerate this talk, but she has to suppress her response until pressure from work eases off. Meanwhile she will sleep alone in the guest bedroom. In Roger's closet she finds his bowling ball in its soft padded bag. It's been at least a year since they've gone bowling. The ball has his name etched on it, as well as the *All American* logo. She kisses the name and places the ball carefully on a pillow at the end of the neck. The three holes look almost like eyes and nose. It rolls side to side on the pillow, as if something about the presence of the body disturbs it. "Yipes," she thinks, "even a bowling ball has feelings." Something like that always makes her wonder. To quiet things down in the bathroom she carefully places the head inside the bowling ball satchel.

"The day was glowing hot, and the scrambling over the rough surface and through the intricate thickets was very fatiguing; but I was well repaid by the strange, Cyclopean scene. As I was walking along I met two large tortoises, each of which must have weighed at least two hundred pounds: one was eating a piece of cactus, and as I approached, it stared at me and slowly stalked away; the other gave a deep hiss, and drew in its head. These huge reptiles, surrounded by the black lava, the leafless shrubs, and large..."

Wrong! She zips it up, and then curious to find out if it still talks while the bag is closed, quickly zips it back down.

"The women, on our first approach, began uttering something in a most dolorous voice, they then squatted themselves down and held up their faces; my companion standing over them, one after another, placed the bridge of his nose at right angles to theirs and commenced pressing. During the process they uttered comfortable little grunts, very much in the same manner as two pigs do, when rubbing against each other. I noticed that the slave..."

Wrong! Talking. Wrong!

She gets up early to head for the office. Almost out the door, she remembers she has neglected to look in on Roger. He always has an especially sweet kiss for her on her way out, and she still wants one. Usually he stays home to write his novel. She runs upstairs to look in the bedroom. The whole sheet now has lifted way off the body, as if being raised to fly from a pole. It makes her think. Unless attached to a brain, the erection does not interest her; but she could appreciate a kiss sans body. She shleps the bag downstairs so the osculation can happen at the familiar threshold. How, she wonders, will the fact that she has to hold up the head affect the kiss? She zips it open. "Sweetheart, I'm off to work."

"Bode's relation may be stated as follows: write down a series of fours; to the first, add zero; to the second, add three; to the third add six equals three times two; to the fourth, twelve equals six times two; to the fifth, twenty-four equals twelve times two, etc; the resulting numbers, divided by ten will give the approximate mean distances of the planets from…"

This is unbearable. "Wrong!" She cries. She zips the bag, and drops it into the closet, next to the umbrellas.

In the cab as she reconstructs the moment she reflects that, unless her eyes have deceived her, Roger's head now appears much smaller than it was when attached, as if it is shrinking away. Everything keeps getting curiouser, but Thursday is still the soonest she'll have time. She puts it from her mind and focuses on work.

The two short morning meetings go well, as does the big board meeting, where she presents her successful strategies to the general approbation of the other execs. She is a kind of hero in the tight inner-management circles of Darkl-Melma Ltd.

So much accomplished in the morning leaves her with a lighter afternoon schedule. She declines the executive lunch. She isn't up to it. As she was making her presentation something strange happened: while she explained some of the graphs, the events of her weekend started to appear to her in images on the screen, then she heard Roger talking, then the sounds of his head separating from his body thundered into her skull. She was well-prepared, and confident enough to muck through the presentation, but now she is shook up. She wants to talk to someone, anyone but another executive. Is she going crazy? Will she cease to function?

She decides to grab a lunch in the employees' cafeteria, where she can be anonymous. One thing she misses from the days she worked in the trenches as a computer operator is casual conversation with other women. Now her lunches are mostly with men, sometimes accompanied by wives or girlfriends, who frequently seem to resent her. Very rarely is there another woman of her rank, and with those there is usually uneasiness, because often there seems to be some tacit competition. What she would like to have back is the coffee breaks or lunches with women— talking salaries, talking husbands and kids, laughing down the harassers in the office, comparing shopping notes, women's problems, dating, friends. She found more good humor, more laughter in the ranks than at the tables of the CEOs.

She leaves her jacket in the office, shakes her hair out of its bun, and unbuttons her blouse a little to let show the tip of the wing of the dragonfly she, in her wilder days, had tattooed above her left breast. Her boyfriend then, Mouse Bernstein, was a tattoo artist, and a Harley freak. Something about Mouse she misses. She gets a bowl of chowder and a Greek salad and sits down in a corner, hoping not to be recognized as the boss, and hoping one of the women will sit down with her.

Before long someone does settle in across the table, with a pasta salad and a peach melba. The woman wipes her spoon and fork with a napkin that she puts in her pocket, and then un-folds another for her lap, tucking the corners under so it makes a hexagon. She smiles at Adeline. The metal braces in her mouth are disturbing, like visual static. Metal braces on older faces make Adeline uneasy because her mom never had money for an orthodontist when she was young, and she grew up think-ing her mouth needed improving. Now that she has the money, she doesn't want to bother; but now, seeing this woman makes her run her tongue across her teeth.

"I'm Sybil from Accounting. I don't think I've seen you in here before. Are you from Customer Service?"

"No. I'm a programmer. My name is Dolores," says Ade-line.

"I thought it was just Customer Service and Accounting in here from one to two. Aren't your people supposed to be eleven to twelve?"

A woman who knows the rules. Adeline likes that. "They made an exception today, because of my problem."

"Pleased to meet you, Dolores." She sucks down a few swirls of rotini. "Which problem is yours?"

"My boyfriend."

"Oh, boyfriend problem."

"Yeah, that one." Adeline swallows a spoonful of chowder, and then starts to speak. "We've been living together more than three years. He's a great guy, a little old-fashioned, a writer; well, not really a writer. He's a novelist. I actually love him a lot. He's sensitive and he's loyal. I don't know. Sometimes we take separate vacations, but we're usually together. Sex is good. It lasts forever." Adeline suddenly feels in her belly she is going to tell too much too fast, but she can't stop herself. "He knows things. Like the history of the forklift, and how it changed warehousing. Sometimes he tells me that. That's good. Isn't that good? He was a forklift operator for years, before he changed his name from Ralph to Roger and became a novelist. We always get along great, until this weekend, and we didn't even argue." Sybil is expressionless. The recessed lighting glints off her braces as she slowly eats. "But I'll tell you, he was doing something to me; I mean, down there, like he does. Usually I like it, but this is going on too long, and I pull on his ponytail to see if I can get him to stop, and something very weird happens." Adeline waits for Sybil to ask what, but her silence continues. "I pull on his ponytail and his head comes off."

The pause is heavy, a moment like a balloon that can't shed its ballast. Nothing rises. Nothing from Sybil. Sweet Roger,

Adeline thinks. She wants to say, "O woe is me. Oy yoy yoy yoy yoy!" Sybil remains expressionless, and Adeline feels the silence packed with monotony. Tears heat her eyes. A fleck of pasta is caught on Sybil's braces.

Sybil asks, "What is his Social Security number, please?"

"I don't know, Sybil. Right now I feel like I'm out here, you know, on the edge of nature, with all the smaller shadows. Shadow of the inch. Spoonshadow. The wild minkshadow. Wee shadows. Of a comma. Shadow of the tampon. But I just held his head up and it was still talking. That's impossible. Wrong! But he was talking. Oy yoy yoy yoy yoy!"

"What is his middle initial? His daytime phone number or a number where he can be reached, like a cell phone or fax number?"

"And then his body was walking around with a big, you know? Everything going into the deeps. Down the well. Shadow of the chestnut. Shadow of moth. Pillshadow." Adeline was earnest, but also enjoyed the words she was starting to talk. She could be the queen of shadows. Or King Shadeline. "It was a big erection. You know, shadow of a tiptoe. Dropshadow. Shadow breathshadow."

"Has he done business with D-M before?"

"I need to find something out. What does the red mean? What happens in the blue?" Adeline brushes a tear from her cheek. "And then when I was working, I started seeing it and hearing him."

"Is this a private or a corporate account? Is there an 800 number? To what address will we send the statement?"

Adeline sees now that the employee is looking into her face as if it was a monitor, and she is waiting for the responses to come up. There is no satisfaction here for Adeline.

Back at her office Adeline succumbs to an invitation to dinner from Eduardo Nifty, CEO of their Perpetual Pet Food division. He has fielded her refusals regularly twice a week for a year-and-a-half and automatically turns to walk away because he can't fathom that he hasn't been rejected this time; so, she has to shout a repeat of her affirmative. She's in no hurry to get home. Quite the opposite. Eduardo is a career executive, with little in his life except his job. They spend a long, boozy evening at the kind of upscale surf-and-turf she never goes to with Roger. Roger is strictly Asian or Middle Eastern vegetable chow. Eduardo's monotonous conversation is not satisfying, but it does relax Adeline.

They leave the restaurant after ten and find separate cabs home. Adeline has yet to prepare a pep talk for the morning meeting with her middle managers. A small piece of work, but it will keep her going till after midnight. Not till the cab pulls away does she realize how tired she is, and her problem with Roger suddenly looms. She takes some comfort that she's a well-known problem solver. She looks up. No lights on in her brownstone, but every room that has a TV—bedroom, living room, even the small black-and-white in the kitchen—someone switched them on and the walls glimmer. How can that be? In the little window of the computer room, modem, fax, CD-ROM library, a screen flickers, in use. In that very room sweet Roger processes his words. Who is using this now? Has Roger's erection unzipped Roger's head? Is a bowling ball playing with her laptop? She fears what she will have to face on the inside, but can't let that stop her.

On other nights she has stepped across the homeless man lying under cardboard cartons across her stoop. No big obstacle. The box covering his uppers has *Do Not Open Until the Millenium* marked on it. She is suddenly enfolded in fear, terror of

42

what is now. She feels vacant, without inner resources. Her life is merely a flicker. Windows glow onto the street.

Adeline backs off to lean against a car and breathes the night air. Tasty. She recognizes something. It's acrid, a hint of sweetness in it, this waft of burning flesh, human burning. She knows that smell from her trip to Bali with Mouse Bernstein. They were there for the cremation season, and for the family they stayed with this was a joyous aroma because they had finally saved enough money to cremate a grandfather and a child, both of whose bodies they had kept in shallow graves 'til they could afford the priest. And she had smelled it again when she first moved back to the city, and the vacant building near her apartment burned almost to the ground. Her cat, out for the night, rubs against her legs and makes a doleful noise. Has Buster been fed? She gazes at the window for a long time. Her fear finally goes away, like a broom on a truck, but she still can't go in. She just can't. She doesn't even want to know what has been going on in there. If ever the aliens in their UFOs are going to come and whisk her away, now's the time. Suddenly, rather like a mudball some kid splats against a window, she is hit by the recognition that she has forgotten how many letters there are in the alphabet. She thinks it's an even number—twenty-two, or twenty-six, or twenty-four. It's in the twenties. Maybe twenty-eight. Or maybe she's wrong, and it's an odd number after all—twenty-five or twenty-seven. Maybe that's wrong and it reaches the thirties. She's quite sure it's not in the teens. That's too few.

She'll recite the whole thing, she decides, and count them each by one; so, she leans her head back against the car and starts from the beginning. "A B C D..." She gets pretty far, all the way to *K*, before she has doubts. She sniffs the air. Still something familiar. She isn't so sure about the J. Maybe she put it in too early. It comes after O, before T. $O\,J\,T\,P$; then she can't remember if N comes first, or M. At least she knows they come together in the sequence, she's pretty sure. $M\,N\,L\,U\,R$? $N\,M\,W$...? $M\,O\,N\,U\,R\,Y$...? $N\,U\,M\,I\,N\,O$...? Numino? Minemony? No. Not two Ns. She pushes ahead with it, and knows it's coming to the end when she hits $L\,U\,W\,Y\,Z\,V\,X$. She's satisfied. X at the end satisfies Adeline.

NELLY HELPS JOE

Joe's big hands spelled trouble at the keyboard. The pads of his fingers were colossal, so that even if he struck the keys perpendicularly, with only the blunt point of each finger, he would register three, or even four letters at once. Even with the point of his jumbo pinky he would hit at least two. Nelly believed Joe could improve with practice if he learned to hold his hands as she showed him, poised above the keyboard, fingers striking lightly straight down. If this practice became habit his skills might increase, in proportion to his increasing understanding. Joe was big, but he wasn't stupid. He easily grasped the nuances of Microsoft Word, at least, conceptually. Other programs, like PowerPoint, or the Adobe family, would not be a problem; at least, conceptually. Nonetheless, his big hands spelled *yertwqreoiuptiyubnvck;ljterw* at the keyboard.

Nelly invested a lot of time and work to teach him. She could sympathize. She liked him. He was big, he was white, he was clumsy. He was brilliant, in his way. He was a third trimester abortion that had failed, thank God; and when he was old enough to understand that—six foot one at the age of eleven— he ran away from his mom, who was relieved finally to be quit of him.

Joe Gargantus' father was a sailor, one of those merchant seamen who spent as little time on shore as possible, because he had no attachments there, and wanted none, and had little respect for the gang of landlubbers that chose to rattle in place on the big island. He preferred life at sea, where there was less to separate you from oblivion, and you could feel your foundations move while you played Omaha and Crib with your mates below deck. He was also a pederast and a pedophile on land, so his son, Joe, was a big mistake, the result of a tedious moment on shore with a woman who took a shine to him while they were waiting in a movie line near Times Square. He was alone, and she was alone. The movie was *Giant*, on a big screen. It starred James Dean. They sat together in the balcony. They got close, then closer. The rest is history—or call it Joe, which is what she calls each of her kids, her dog, her houseplants, and her current boyfriend. It's convenient when all is Joe. Joe's father never knew about him, though he might have enjoyed Joe's company when he was a six-year-old, before he really started to grow.

Of course, Nelly Mishbooker didn't know any of this about Joe Gargantus. If she had it might have pushed her sympathies even further, and who knows what she would have done then for him; whereas now she gave him some special attention, trying to get him to orient his big hands correctly over the keyboard, and she never let him give in to his frustration and would stay with him a little longer, past the ninety minutes of the class, but this was nothing she wouldn't have done for any of her students with special problems.

In fact, Joe didn't know this about himself, and the idea that he might have had a father somewhere hardly ever crossed his mind. When once he saw a picture of James Dean in a Sunday magazine story, he felt a slight perturbation, and made a mental note that he might rent those movies some time; but that he might connect this actor with his own conception, or think that James Dean might be his father? Unlikely.

Melinda, his mom, didn't know the whole story either. At the time of Joe's conception his father was watching the movie over her shoulder while she listened from his lap. She saw the light stream widen out of the projector window. She sucked at names. A sailor. Joe. Maybe he said Gargantus. What the hell?

Nelly Mishbooker was raised in a sharecropper's shack in South Carolina. Her father was a white boy who took advantage of her mother almost daily for a whole summer as she walked home in the evening from Fiona Mishbooker's estate, where she did housecleaning and gardening. The white boy was Mrs. Mishbooker's son, Beeper, who became a state senator, then lieutenant governor, then ran for the U.S. Senate and almost won. He was the force behind the drive to change the colors of all the roadsigns in the state and, by God, they were changed. Of course, he denied his paternity; so although Nelly knew her father was a Mishbooker, it did her little good. She took the name for her own in later life just because it seemed the spiteful thing to do. Perhaps these circumstances made for a special mysterious bond between herself and Joe, that semiorphanhood that they tacitly could recognize in each other. Nelly's stepfather, Cyrus Ophilus Mackenzie, persecuted her because she was so fair-skinned. "Mulatto, out of my sight," he would say, and he'd call her spawn of the devil. He was a deacon at the Third Fundamental Church of The Christ Arising. Because of him she left home at thirteen, another coincidence that she and Joe never discussed.

With a little good luck and a lot of perseverance throughout her young life Nelly managed to get through school, and finally took a degree in computer science. She had a special aptitude for keeping in her head, as if in discrete compartments, all the popular word processing and spreadsheet programs, as well as PageMaker and publishing programs, Adobe Photoshop, several complicated architectural design programs, and more. People who knew her work said that Nelly Mishbooker had a three-thousand-gigabyte head. She was skillful enough as a programmer to be able to write programs customized for individual clients. In short, she was a nerd and a whiz.

For solving Joe's problem, which was purely mechanical, she had almost too much skill; but it was the simplicity and physicality of it that attracted her. His difficulty was basic hardware clumsiness. She liked hardware problems because they made her feel more substantial. One of the minuses she had to accept in her profession was a frustration arising from how difficult it was to be real, really *real* in the world while working with computers.

It came to pass as time went by that Joe's attention to Nelly's instruction turned to an attention to Nelly herself. Because of his size he was aware of how he could intimidate, so he was always very careful, particularly when addressing small women. Nonetheless he managed one day, as the lesson was ending, to ask in his smallest, shyest voice, "Is it...what...are you having any plans for dinner?"

This surprised Nelly, because he had never before spoken to her personally. Her habits were cool, however, and nothing ever really shook her up. This came from years of living black in a white world, and fair-skinned in a black world. Prejudice from every side gave her a certain cool, an automatic delayed reaction.

"I'd be glad to," she said after a long moment battling her own rule against socializing with students.

"Good," Joe grinned. It was the biggest grin she'd ever seen. This made Joe so happy that he relaxed onto three chairs, and embraced five keyboards at once. Nothing that came up on the screens made any sense, until the winged toasters flew again.

At Angelo's Pizzeria, Joe confessed to her that he was a poet. She sat across from him in a booth that was narrow enough so that when she looked at him, even if she pressed the back of her head against the back of the booth, Nelly couldn't see all of him at once.

"I'm writing," he said. "A long poem about the history of Colorado Springs. That's where I grew up, though I'm not sure I really ever grew up; anyway, that's where I got to full size. I wasn't born there. I was born in New Hampshire."

"Did you like it there?" Nelly asked. To her, Colorado Springs was a spooky town, with all its military bases, the Air Force Academy, and Cheyenne Mountain hollowed out for the national defense nerve center and apocalypse survival complex. And then in the center of the town there was that little human- ist school, Colorado College and all its sensitive people, like a drop of honey surrounded by a huge suicide pill.

"I don't even know if I liked it," Joe said. "Maybe when I finish this poem I'll know."

"I always thought," Nelly said, reaching across to touch Joe's arm, "that the weirdest thing about living in Denver was that Rocky Flats and all that plutonium was just a few miles away, and that Colorado Springs and all that death was two hours down the road."

"Less, when I drive," Joe said, then he said something pe- culiar, he said, "The pain-people think God is the god of joy,

/ the joy-people think that God is the god of pain / the coast dwellers think that love is in the mountains, / and the mountain dwellers think that love is at the seashore so they go down to the sea."

"What is that?" Nelly asked.

"It's a poem," said Joe.

"Did you write it?"

"No. I wish. It's by a poet from Israel."

"What does it mean?"

"I don't know. It means what it says. That wasn't the whole poem, anyway. I just like pain-people and joy-people."

"You know it by heart?"

Joe grinned. "Heart is essential."

Nelly was surprised at how little Joe ate, just two slices of a medium pizza. She ate four before she knew it, and felt like a big pig. She picked it up with her hands, but he cut it rather daintily on his plate, and ate it in neat little portions with knife and fork. The utensils looked in his hands as if they'd come from a dollhouse.

"So I guess," said Nelly, after they finished the pizza, "that you want to learn the computer to help you write your poem."

"I can't write on a computer. I need to write with a pencil, on a legal pad."

"Then why learn computer?"

"Because I'm afraid of it."

The idea that one so big could be afraid of anything was another surprise for Nelly. He could tear a computer in two with his bare hands. A lot of her students were afraid of computers because they had to learn a new language, and they didn't like to look stupid, or maybe they just didn't like to make mistakes. But Joe seemed to mean something different.

"Next time I'll cook you dinner," she said, without planning to say it. She wasn't even sure he could fit through the door of her apartment.

When Nelly told her aerobics buddy, Jasmine, about how big Joe was, she really got her attention. Jasmine was a tall, muscular woman herself, with good pecs, long, sinewy legs, and small breasts. She fanatically kept her body in shape.

"Just how big is this big man, Nelly?"

Nelly tried to describe him by standing on her tiptoes and forming his body with her arms outstretched. Jasmine's copper-colored eyes opened wide as the circle of her mouth that was changing shape on her face. "O, wow! It really makes you wonder."

"But despite all his size, he really seems delicate, almost dainty. He's a poet, but he looks like he could tear people into shreds."

Jasmine pulled the Lycra away from her chest, as if to release steam. "I'd get curious. Don't you get curious?"

"He's a really sensitive person."

"I mean, do you think he's that big all over? Is everything in proportion?" She made a face.

"He wants to learn computers, but his fingers are so big he can't press just one key at a time."

"Do you think all his parts are that big?"

"But I think I've got this idea that will solve his problem. When he comes over for dinner I'll... What do you mean, all his parts?"

"Well do you think his, you know..."

"Jasmine, is that all you ever think about?"

STEVE KATZ

Jasmine shrugged. "I'm not thinking about anything. I'm just curious, like any grown woman; I mean, what if...? You can do the research."

"I'm trying to help this guy. He's a poet, a writer. He needs to be able to use a computer, and he's almost disabled, computer-wise; at least, he's dimensionally disadvantaged."

"But you have to take into account his assets, too," Jasmine said, mischievously.

"I'm a computer teacher," Nelly said, proudly.

"Well, yeah, but if you find out about that other, just let me know. Send me an email." They went back onto the aerobics floor. "I would do that for you," said Jasmine, as she brought a knee to her chin.

Joe's frustration at the computer was eased now due to the special attention and optimism of his teacher. She had assuaged most of his computer angst. His big project, to spell out in rhymed couplets the history of Colorado Springs, would become much easier to revise once he had the skills. And it wasn't that he didn't understand the word processing programs, but that he just covered too much equipment with one fell swoop. He was still a human being, no matter what, and would find a solution. It was for a similar reason that he washed out of dental school, because the picks and drills were too tiny for his hands, and his fingers were too big to fit in anybody's mouth.

He snapped open the case of his laptop and touched the switch with a pencil. It was a colorful, friendly display, that when it booted carried the message, "You're the new whiz, Joe!" Nelly always snuck a motivational message onto his screen. He looked at his legal pad, and painstakingly tapped out with a pencil a

few lines from his poem, just to see how they looked:

> Of Colorado Springs I sing to you
> Where flyboys prance, and cowboys too.
> And Zebulon Pike, whose peak is priceless,
> Welcomes all hikers, when the trails are iceless.

It was good to see it on the screen. The lines seemed to vibrate there with new energy. He was modeling this poem after an obscure book he found in a library in Boulder, Colorado. It was called *THE FUNNY PLACE*, which was a history of Coney Island written in rhymed couplets by Richard Snow, and published by an equally obscure press called Adventures In Poetry. Once he finished his book, which he thought he'd call, *THE SCARY PLACE*, in homage to his model, he was going to send it to Adventures In Poetry, to its editor, Larry Fagin, who was for Joe Gargantus a hero of the world of poetry.

And Joe had new energy from working with Nelly Mishbooker. He wasn't prepared to like someone as much as he found himself liking her. It was as if she had become his muse, personal unto himself. No one could motivate him the way she did. He wanted to tell her he would go to any end of the earth for her.

Dinner at her place had its awkward moments, however, as when she tried not to stare at him stooping and squeezing through her doorway, or when she realized at the table he wouldn't fit into the armchair she had placed there for him. She didn't know what to do. It was her biggest chair. Then she remembered she had a bench in her spare room that she had kept when she sold her piano, narrow but long enough so he could spread out on it, and eat in his dainty way a bit of the curried eggplant and a small portion of turbot poached in Madeira and bayberry oil. The salad going into his mouth looked like bats diving into a nightclub.

When they finished eating he leaned back and said, "Complacencies of the peignoir, and late / Coffee and oranges in a sunny chair, / And the green freedom of a cockatoo / Upon a rug mingle to dissipate / The holy hush of ancient sacrifice…"

She couldn't be absolutely sure, but she thought he was speaking poetry. So when he asked questions like, "Why should she give her bounty to the dead?" or, "Where, then, is paradise?" or "Is there no change of death in paradise?" or "Why set the pear upon those river banks?" (*why, indeed?* Nelly thought), she didn't feel she needed to answer. She thought it was poetry because the only time you mention paradise so much is in poetry, or in preaching or advertising, and she knew it wasn't advertising, and it didn't sound completely like a sermon. She liked the music in some of the words he said, like, "We live in an old chaos of the sun." No one had ever said that to her before, and she didn't see a reason to disagree. And when he said, "At evening, casual flocks of pigeons make / Ambiguous undulations as they sink, / Downward to darkness on extended wings," she almost fainted. It must have been the "ambiguous undulations."

She sighed and gathered herself back together. He watched her, the biggest grin in the world on his face. He liked the way she listened to his telling poetry, and she liked the way he told it to her, though a lot of it passed right through her circuits without registering a meaning. "I am writing now of preconceptions / Those of sex and ropes." The sound was nice, however, and his voice a smooth river of syllables. Then all at once it got silent, and one of those moments opened that can be excruciating when people are becoming acquainted, when no one has a thing to say, and all of a sudden the room shrinks around them and someone looks for the nearest TV remote, or for evidence of a computer so you can start a software conversation. This was a moment like those in which during the years before AIDS lust might have flown in through the window like a fresh Holstein flung by a tidal wave.

Then Nelly got up and Joe watched her go into the other room, and he thought, *What a nice dinner she prepared for me. So rare that someone cooks a dinner for anyone anymore. Maybe she likes me. I would do anything for her.*

Nelly came out of the room, holding something behind her back. "Joe," she said. "I've been thinking a lot about your problem, and I hope I've come up with an idea."

She placed in front of his face the package she'd been hiding behind her back. He gasped. His eyes flew wide open and he covered them with his hands. He wanted to run away as fast as he could as far as he could to the North, or else put on every one of them that the package contained, every one he could, and embrace Nelly, and hold her till she turned to porridge. She was showing him a package of five dozen condoms, a sixty-pack. That was what she put before him. What could this mean? Sweat rained down from his palms, his mouth watered, his eyesight blurred, he blushed all over.

"See, my thought is…"

He interrupted her. "Nelly, I like you in an enormous way, but shouldn't we… I mean, isn't it too soon? Shouldn't we go for a walk first, or bake brownies together, or… I don't know what to say. And you're my teacher. This is dangerous. They'll take away your library privileges, the key to the faculty bathroom. They'll make you sleep in a wetsuit."

"It's not what you think, Joe. Listen to me," she said. "You are right that these are condoms, or safes, or buster baggies, whatever you like to call them, but my idea is that you should try to use them on your fingers."

Joe looked at his fingers.

"See, each one of these will stretch over one of your fingers, I think, and at the end of each one is a little reservoir. Into each of the reservoirs you can fit a pencil eraser that you've shaped to a point, and once you get used to it you strike the keys with those erasers rather than those big galoots of fingers that you've got. You'll be processing the words as fast as anyone."

Joe saw that Nelly was proud of this solution she'd devised. Although he had embarrassed himself a little with his original assumptions, he accepted her gift and thanked her. He broke the erasers off some pencils she gave him, sharpened them a little with a penknife, worked them into the reservoirs of the condoms, then stretched the condoms over his fingers. They both got a laugh at his clumsiness when, because he was still wearing the prophylactics, he misjudged grabbing the serving spoon and sank his fingers directly into the tiramisu. The feeling of kinship between them was very close to love. He could hardly talk to her any more except to say as he left, "This is just to say / I have eaten / the plums / that were in / the icebox / and which / you were probably / saving / for breakfast / Forgive me / they were delicious / so sweet / and so cold."

She thought about that a lot once Joe was gone. It must have been a poem, what he said, although it didn't really sound like one. She thought about the plums. What did plums have to do with it? Did they rhyme with condoms? It was nice. He was very nice. But plums were puzzling.

Joe went right home. He wore the condoms all the way, because he wanted to start practicing as soon as he got to his laptop. In a few weeks the class would be over, finishing with a contest that pitted the students against each other for speed and accuracy. He thought the best way he could show his appreciation would be to win that contest.

Nelly agreed to meet Jasmine at The Newsstand Café on the corner of Sixth and Washington. Over the phone, Jasmine told her she was planning a big change in her life, and she needed to talk it over with her friend. It was warm for early December, a nice morning. The skiff of snow that had accumulated overnight was already history. The air was clear. The traffic on Sixth looked elegant in December light. In the café people were lined up to buy newspapers and get their lattes to go, on the way to work. They looked grand, these people in their spotless suits, alert and charged up, ready for new challenges at the office. Jasmine was already sitting at a table next to the birthday card display, reading the *New York Times*, when Nelly arrived. She got some coffee and sat down across from her friend. Jasmine folded up her paper, and grinned.

"So what is it?" Nelly asked.

"My aunt Tuffy died."

"Tuffy?"

"That was her nickname, because she'd always say, 'I think I'll go sit on a tuffet.'"

"I'm sorry about that."

"Oh, it's okay. I hardly even knew her, but she left me some money."

"That's great."

"I think I'll move to Seattle."

"Why? You just moved here."

"I've been here two years, already. But I can get my teaching certificate there, and I know I like the ocean. I loved *Sleepless In Seattle*."

Nelly spotted something on the page of the *New York Times* that had fallen in front of her. It was the Religion page, and in a small box towards the bottom was advertised a week of revival meetings outside of Philadelphia with the up and coming pair of televangelists, Cyrus Ophilus Mackenzie, and Rafael (Beeper) Mishbooker, of the Third Baptist Church of The Revelations, Internet. The former was the name of her stepfather, and the latter, of course, was her real father's name. He had made the shift from politics to the pulpit. Mishbooker, man of God. It snatched her breath away, festered in her mind. She started to ponder things she'd long ago forgotten.

"So what do you think?" Jasmine asked. She waited for an answer, then raised her voice, "Nelly! Yoo-hoo. Hello." She waved her hand in front of Nelly's face.

"Oh, I think it's good. Go to Seattle. Yes. Tuffy."

"I bet I know what's up."

Nelly looked at Jasmine, "What?"

"You saw it. You got a look at your big friend's thing. A good look, I bet."

"Jasmine."

"Don't be coy, girlfriend. How big is it?" Jasmine leaned almost all the way across the table.

"Yes, big. Okay?"

"Tell me about it."

Nelly looked down at the paper again, transfixed by the names in bold type.

"Tell your girlfriend. How big?" Jasmine spread her arms as if showing the measure of a big fish.

"He could tear people apart."

"ALL RIGHT." Jasmine made a fist and jerked it into her body. "Tell me. Tell all."

"With his bare hands," Nelly mused.

"And?... Hup... What?"

"It was a religious experience, okay?"

Jasmine threw her arms up and whooped so loud she startled the young lawyer at the cream dispenser. He spilled the white stuff across his brand new kangaroo-hide dispatch case.

Joe spent almost all his time during this period working at his laptop, getting down the little strokes, so he got faster and faster. He had almost no time to work on *The Scary Place*, and he missed that a lot, but frequently while he was at work in the Checker Auto Parts Store, where he would long ago have been manager if his fingers were smaller, a couplet would come to him like, "At Cheyenne Mountain they've got the plan / That helps them survive the destruction of man." And he would stop whatever he was doing and write it down on anything handy— invoice, register roll, napkin from the 7-Eleven. He stuffed these in his pockets and threw them into a box when he got home.

At the classes in the evening he barely exchanged glances with Nelly. She'd ask him how he was getting along with the new system, and he'd show her, and she'd encourage him. Of course, she was busy. Since it was the last couple of weeks of the class all the students were making sure they got as much information and help as they could. She even neglected to sneak those en- couraging messages that used to appear when he booted up at home. The exception was two days before the final contest. It was a Tuesday. He had to work at noon the next day, so decided to stay up after the class and practice for an hour or two. He booted up at home, and finally there was a message from Nelly. He had to boot up twice before he could believe what it said, and then he booted it again.

"Could you kill somebody, Joe?"

An interrogative. It was the first time she'd ever put a question on his screen. It was the only thing on there. Maybe it wasn't from Nelly, but it had to be. "Could you kill somebody, Joe?" He couldn't wipe it off. He couldn't even shut it off. It was from Nelly. No doubt of it. But he couldn't stay in the room with this. He went to the living room and sat down on the couch. The message had made him sweat. He needed a different couch, a new one. This one had collapsed. He suddenly had the urge to call his mother. He hadn't ever talked to her since the day he ran away, but he did have a picture of her that his sister, Joe, sent him a few years back. That was the last time he'd heard from anyone in his family. She told him their mom was living in Seattle, with some guy named Joe. She must have been pretty old by now, in her fifties at least.

It surprised him how easy it was to get her number from directory assistance, and how quickly she picked up when he called.

"Yeah," she said.

He hesitated, then, "Hello," said Joe.

"Who is this?" she asked.

"It's Joe."

"Joe who?"

"Joe Gargantus, your son."

"I got no son, Joe."

"Big Joe, you remember. It's been a long time."

"Oh, big Joe. My son. How you doing? I thought you were dead."

"I'm not. I'm alive."

His mother grunted, and he started to tell her his whole story, how when he left he got a job cleaning stables at a race-track outside of Tucson and saved some money there and went east to Pittsburgh with the driver of a truck full of horses and then got a job there in a shoe factory picking up scraps and then running a cutter, and made quite a bit of money. Then he got tired of Pittsburgh and went east with a small carnival that played county fairs all over the East Coast. He lived in a trailer with Henry Henrietta the hermaphrodite sideshow feature, and worked some of the rides and concessions because he was big and intimidating. By then he was sixteen, and he left the carnival in New York state, and hitched up to Maine, and then all the way to Halifax, in Canada, where he got work in the galley of one of the last tramp steamers. It sailed under an Ethiopian flag, but was manned by Malays and Portugese. That was the worst job. At every port they locked him in his cabin, in every country. He jumped ship finally, when they got back to the U.S., a call in Providence, Rhode Island, where inspectors went through the ship, heard him yelling, and made the mates release him. He jumped off the lee side of the ship, swam to the wharf, and didn't stop running for a whole day. All this time he had been studying all the subjects on his own and in Rhode Island took his high school equivalency test, and passed it with great marks. Surprisingly, the shipping company had deposited his pay all along into an account in Halifax, and that, with his savings in Pittsburgh and Albany, gave him enough money to get a start in college. So he went on a special program for the orphaned and indigent to Brown University, and got a good education there, and easy admission to the Rhode Island College of Dentistry, where his luck ran out. His size caught up with him there, and he washed out in confusion.

He didn't remember at what point in his monologue his mother had hung up, but he went on telling the story even after he got a peculiar message, "You have reached a number that has been disconnected. If you'd like to place another call, please hang up and try again."

Telling his whole story to his mom exhausted him, but also made him feel very light and relieved. "I've got a story. I am the story," he congratulated himself. He went back to his desk and hit a key to dissipate the screen saver. Another message appeared:

"Joe. Would you do it for me?"

At the closing ceremony of their computer course all the students received certificates. The contest was no big deal, but Joe did well enough. He couldn't keep up with Peggy Baca, who had gobbled up computer info like a duck after breadcrumbs; but he came in second. Peggy got the modem, but he was happy with his free Internet hours, and he always knew he would have won the modem if he hadn't been so hasty putting on his finger aids. The eraser on his right ring finger kept folding under.

Nelly was dressed up for the occasion, and looked exceptionally beautiful in an aqua crepe mini with gray mesh stockings and Swedish clogs. Her blouse was a rosy flounce, and through the cut of her sleeves you could see some of her breast when she half-lifted her arm. Joe had never seen her with her eyes done so carefully. He looked great himself. He had gone to the Big and

Tall shop, because he was both, and had got himself a soft black and gray checked sport jacket, and dark chocolate brown flannel pants, and a pinkish button-down shirt, and a narrow green paisley tie, and these new clothes made him seem a little smaller, the way they contained him. He was very handsome.

Nelly hugged him openly and with affection when she gave him his runner-up prize, and through the evening she kept touching him and taking his hand, as if she didn't care any longer now that the class was over.

When he received his award all his classmates were surprised that he stood up to speak, because during the four month course he had said very little, and that only in the most constrained and high-pitched tones, as if he wanted to deny his size with the tiniest voice. But he spoke now in the kind of deep, gong-like tones you might expect from such a giant. He declaimed in a voice that filled the whole room, "I've got a story. I am the story." Then he lifted his hands that looked like ghosts with the fingers festooned in condoms and erasers, and proclaimed, "I am the story electric!"

Because no one had an inkling this romance was going on, all the students were shocked as Nelly left the ceremony with Joe, bouncing up to kiss him as they went out the door. In the cab on the way to her house she kissed him again and again, on his face and his hands, and then pulled from her pink purse—the inside looked like the gut of a big sea anemone—a blue envelope, out of which she slid, just to let him see it, two tickets to Philadelphia, on United, leaving in the morning from Denver International Airport.

HOLLYWOOD NOVELETTE

CAST OF CHARACTERS
and
glossary

(in order of appearance)

Agnes : Andrew Warhola
Eukan Severe : Keanu Reeves
Dojie Resoft : Jody Foster
Monisantaca : Santa Monica
Necsgreems : Screen Gems
Maslygdnow : Sam Goldwyn
emrafs : frames
Bysbu Kleebrey : Busby Berkeley
Plinach : Chaplin
Blimclecledie : Cecil B. DeMille
Leinvojeeseph : Joseph E. Levine
dreulasis : residuals
Etatreh : Theater
Slegeslona : Los Angeles
Sgronts Respute : Preston Sturges
Ildrew Libly : Billy Wilder
Yinlaw Sted : Walt Disney
Clenac Jectorp : cancel project
Nonawi Erryd : Winona Ryder
Verri Hoxnepi : River Phoenix
Glasoud : Douglas
Chamiel's : Michael's
Tanoke : Keaton
Ajieck Nach : Jackie Chan
Onatint Taurda : Antonin Artaud

Naanittor : Tarantino
Tenquin : Quentin
Sterub : Buster
Turb Scalranet : Burt Lancaster
Yerml Perset : Meryl Streep
Sitund Monfahf : Dustin Hoffman
cartnoct : contract
Thyka Abset : Kathy Bates
Sorb Imulrèe : Lumière Bros.
Nealsty Burkick : Stanley Kubrick
Lenoci Mindak : Nicole Kidman
Dr. Deppster Johnjon : Dr. Deppster Johnjon
phroa : Oprah
Negger : Negger
Hitchfred Alcock : Alfred Hitchcock
stagnir : ratings
yonoletenus : Looney Tunes
milfrion : film noir
treepflak : Peter Falk
arazazipp : paparazzi
lacopani : Al Pacino
lamar-spleam : Marla Maples
Lohly Uhrent : Holly Hunter
progs : progenitors
Ornash Sento : Sharon Stone
Gme Yran : Meg Ryan
Xupset Fron : upfront sex
Noride : DeNiro
Thwyneg Trowlap : Gwyneth Paltrow
Trober : Robert
Shonirra Drof : Harrison Ford

Borter Lalvud : Robert Duvall
Ronyalmy : Myrna Loy
Ralck Algelb : Clark Gable
Tighovnoj : Jon Voight
Kerpar Yespo : Parker Posey
Mediroome : Demi Moore
Crubeliwlis : Bruce Willis
Ryga Yesbu : Gary Busey
Theki Dracanire : Keith Carradine
Tocst Nengl : Scott Glenn
Bybob Lawrek : Bobby Walker
Rylinma Noorem : Marilyn Monroe
Mau Ruthnam : Uma Thurman

NOT DEAD NOT JIMMY STEWART NOT ROBERT MITCHUM
DO NOT DIE IN HOLLYWOOD NOT DEAD NOT JIMMY ST
EWART NOT ROBERT MITCHUM DO NOT DIE IN HOLLYW

AGNES
(the auto-autobiography)
the protocols of the martyrs of fashion
a tale of glamour, family values, and cannibalism

(Please note: all the events described below are actual. Only the names have been changed to protect the somnolent. Any resemblance to persons living or dead is purely sentimental.)

Eukan Severe was a dutiful son. He neither understood nor condoned the rebellious posturings of his sister, Dojie Resoft. She was sixteen, almost seventeen, two years older than himself. He hoped he might get to understand her better as he reached her age. They lived in a comfortable, fading, split-level house in an old suburb of the town of Monisantaca, at the north end of the lush Plinach valley, in the westernmost reaches of the Necsgreems province. The town is bisected by the Maslygdnow river fed by runoff from the snowy slopes of the Bysbu Kleebrey volcano. The river is less than four *emrafs* wide at this point, but quite deep. Further south it widens, enriched by snow melt off the Blimclecledie range. There it joins the mighty Leinvojeeseph, usually called The Line. Along the banks of this mighty river the people of the plains cultivate and defend their *dreulasis* crops, the mildly narcotic tuberous staple they learned to grow from the Etatreh peoples. These are original inhabitants, who survive only in secluded enclaves, and still exert their influence despite campaigns to wipe them out, through neglect, if not through slaughter. The Line broadens over the plains, with many branches and culs-de-sac that make up the waterways that lace the urban sprawl of Slegeslona. Further south the river dives deep under a parched expanse of desert, to seep up again after many miles, forming the steamy bog the old people call Sgronts Respute. Then it gathers again to meander the Ildrew Libly rain forest, until it flows into the sea through the fertile delta on which Yinlaw Sted is built.

We present this brief topography only to give you a picture of the scale of the adventure that awaited Eukan as a result of his obsession, since age twelve, with building a boat in the manner of the Etatreh people, a small boat designed to travel this river. This, and the urging of his sister who feared for his life, started Eukan on an adventure well beyond his years. Dojie felt she had to defend her brother against their parents, who she could tell were about to enter their first period of voracity. This is a common affliction that comes at least once to every married couple. At a certain point in their relationship they feel compelled to devour their oldest son. They can't control this, and many who have suffered by their successes explain to the commission that monitors this behavior that there was no way they could stop themselves. This period in a marriage is called *pünkscheit*. Some who marry young and bear their first son at a young age put themselves in danger because the kid might have already reached the age of seventeen, or eighteen, and be physically powerful, and aware of what was happening, and try to dispose of his progenitors with his fists, elbows, knees, or with his *clenac jectorp*, a sacramental saber he inherits from his maternal grandfather when he passes his sixteenth birthday. Although there is an old statute on the books, criminalizing *pünksheit*, this is never prosecuted with much vigor. Except for the one powerless commission, made up mostly of scientists, the community more or less ignores the practice. After all, the people reason, abortion is illegal. We can't make everything illegal. And they rationalize further that in this case the boy is absorbed back into the flesh of its parents, who often conceive another boy, and that boy is frequently an improvement; in fact, the school rosters and other such lists accounting for attendance, register a big *R* next to the name of a boy so disappeared, *R* for *Reabsorbed*.

Eukan was too young, Dojie told herself, to slush out what was going on, and because of his sweet nature, he wasn't inclined to oppose the will of their parents. Dojie had already overheard their parents engage in the re/amorous conversations that precede *pünkscheit*. She knows all about it because her friend, Nonawi Erryd, who had lost her brother, Verri Hoxnepi, to their parents' voracity, told her about all the warning signs. Nonawi loved her brother, an older one who taught her how to dance, and how to do many drashy things, like stick a skewer through her neck, and she didn't want Dojie to suffer a similar loss. Parents were a problem, drooped and gruelly, and neither girl ever wanted to become one ever.

"So where did your brother go now?" insisted Yerml Perset, Dojie's mother. "Where did you say?"

"I didn't say anything," Dojie replied curtly. "What makes you think I should know anything about where he goes?" She was cleaning her lateral action skates. She had just bought this new pair of Glasoud Rollers at Chamiel's, and she loved them more than anything. The feeling of sideways skating was pure drash.

"He's never around any more. He used to help me with the housework all the time." Her mother took the wine glasses out of the dishwasher, and held them up to the light. "You're the only one, practically, who talks to him any more. You'd think he didn't even know he had a mom and dad. And we love him, just as we did when he was a little baby. We love him from his sweet little feet, through his bellybutton, to the tip of his nose."

"Yeah, right." Another sure sign of *pünkscheit*—Non-awi had told her—was the conceptual reinfantilization of the boy, followed often by the demented logic that interpreted the devouring as a reabsorption and reformation of the kid's substance into something more compatible with the parents' original wishes. Sick. Was there no one sweeter than Eukan? What about him could they ever want to change? This was even sicker, Dojie thought, than the postpartum dream some women have where they eat their babies back into their wombs. It was sick. In general, life was sick. All she wanted to do was side-skate down along the river and meet her friends. At least they were friends.

Her mother read her mind.

"Before you go out, young lady." Dojie retreated from putting on her skates because she knew what her mother was going to say. "You fold the rest of your laundry and put it away, and it wouldn't hurt for you to clean up your room a little. It looks like a twister hit."

"I like it the way it is."

"Like some kind of muck-artist's studio?"

Dojie put down her skates and squeezed past her mother to go into the laundry room. Sometimes obedience was the path of least resistance. Yerml grabbed her by her shoulders and planted a kiss on her cheek. "Sorry if I'm short with you, sweety. I just worry about Eukan. Can't you just tell us where he goes? We' ve hardly seen him for three days."

Dojie recoiled. A kiss from her mother was too much affection. "No. I said I've got nothing to tell you. I don't know anything."

"Please. This isn't like him."

"I don't know where he is, and even if I did I would not tell you."

"Why, sweety? I'm his mom."

"Right. *Pünkscheit*, plain and simple."

"That…! Do you believe that old story?"

Of course, her mother was denying it. "It's not an old story, mom," Dojie sang.

Dojie wasn't lying. She actually didn't know where her brother was, but she did know he had gone into the mountains to escape and think things over, and she wasn't going to tell the progenitors that. He decided this was a good time to see if he could find the high valley where the last of the Tanoke trees grew. The disappearance of these trees is another sad story of exploitation of natural resources, and wasting of a valuable and beautiful species. At one time the whole northern range was sheltered in the grace of these unique trees. They grow up to a hundred and forty feet in height, and produce only two broad leaves at the very top, with a seedpod growing from a spike between them. The leaves are tough and resilient, at the same time they are light and buoyant. When sliced across their breadth they exude an opalescent juice that dries to a powder varying in hue from rose-pink to aquamarine, and that is iridescent in a certain angle of light. This powder at one time became a cosmetic rage in Monisantaca, and when it invaded the huge, sophisticated market of Slegeslona the demand became so great that greed encouraged the hurried and careless harvesting of these leaves. By the time the fad had passed, most of the trees were dead. When in the old times the Etatreh peoples harvested the leaves, to construct their sturdy boats, they always waited till the right time for the tree, when the seed pod was fully mature, and they cut the leaves at a precise moment, just before the tree was ready to launch its pod. A moment after the launch the leaves dropped to the ground useless and spent, retaining none of their valuable qualities, and the tree went through a period of dormancy, before it produced its new leaves. The Etatrehs knew there was this safe period, when it was right to take the leaves, without ruining the tree. They assigned one of themselves to watch each tree they were going to harvest, and with this care they almost never killed one; but if by some mistake they did, they performed a ritual of remorse, an incantation of regret. The tree was part of the whole envelope of their lives, and therefore part of their flesh.

Eukan knew these incantations, he knew the rituals, at least as he and his best friend, Ajieck Nach, learned them from the writings of Onatint Taurda, one of their idols. They'd also found on the Informator the instructions for building the boat the Etatrehs made from these leaves. To stitch them properly he knew he'd have to find the nest of the now-rare Sterub spider. It wasn't totally clear what he'd need from it, perhaps its web; but he did know he'd have to solicit its help. Ajieck and he had even practiced the protocols of solicitation, which they'd learned from swimming the Informator.

The only thing he regretted, on leaving for the mountains, was not telling Ajieck or his own sister. He wasn't used to doing things without at least their knowing about it; and Ajieck and himself planned and did almost everything together. But this he had to do alone. It was stressful enough to keep from getting his parents' permission; in fact, he knew it was against their wishes, because they had been getting weird about wanting to keep him close to them all the time. He had to do it alone, didn't want anyone else to have to take any of the blame.

The first day he made good time, leaving from the center of the city through a network of alleys he knew really well, so he wouldn't be noticed by anyone. He slogged through the Naanittor swamp so as to avoid most of the 'burbs where he might be spotted, and then he climbed away into the shadows on the sheerest Tenquin scarpment, so there would be almost no chance for anyone to see him at all. By the time he stopped to eat some dried fruit and vegetable crackers, Monisantaca was behind him, and ahead of him were the steep foothills of the Turb Scalranset mountain range. He climbed throughout the rest of the afternoon, then made camp in a small clearing near a brook, using survival skills he had learned from his father, to make a small lean-to, a comfortable bed of leaves, and to build a small fire on which he could roast a mess of golden faxberries, that were plentiful late in the summer. He had learned all this from his dad. As he settled his head onto a pillow of moss, his loneliness weighed down on him. He missed everyone, his sister and Ajieck most of all, but also his dad, and his mom. He shouldn't have done this. Rumors of *pünkscheit* were no excuse for disobedience, even if they were true. That they were intending to make him into a feast? Ridiculous. Not his mom. Not his dad. He would pay for this rebellion some- how; he knew that. His shoulders ached. He wished he were home. He was one blob of tired muscle and bone, and how his head thromped. What good was his life if he didn't live it cor- rectly, honoring his parents? He turned to the side, so the tears could slip down his cheeks. He would go back. In the morning, he would do something. He had the feeling that people often get alone at night in the woods, and with good reason, that something out there was watching him. His sobs slowly soft- ened into breathing, and his breath into dreams.

Yerml Perset began to feel better about herself once she became a volunteer. The sense of purposelessness and the futil- ity of life that had oppressed her forever slowly dissipated as she began to work in the community. It was a surprise. She had promised herself early on, when she was Dojie's age, never to become one of those pitiful do-gooders whose lives seemed so artificial, those docents and social chairladies. She wasn't yet even close to the blue-rinse stage, but she surprised herself with the gobs of energy she could grab from doing service in the community. This was about being out there, testing new skills, redeploying old ones, meeting new people. Informator sales out of her home brought in good money, but never did this for her, never made her feel like a part of Monisantaca. This was the start of a whole new phase of her life that really changed her attitude towards everything, even towards Sitund Monfahf, her dear husband. For a long time she had in her depression indulged in self-pity about the dullness of their long marriage, the sexual apathy, the tedious, predictable arguments,

STEVE KATZ

the futurelessness; but now, suddenly, they were rediscovering each other, and exploring previously untapped aspects of each other's sensuality, and she was finding new joy in eroticizing parts of him she'd never noticed before, like the nob just below the back of his wrist, and a shadow that in certain light spread under the center of his lower lip. She wanted to squeeze his chin with her knees, oh, and his ears, which she had not ever enjoyed before, she wanted to fold them both out like outriggers, if only his head could flatten that way; and she would love to hide each of her nipples in one of those little sweetie-flaps. There was an upwelling of feeling for her children as well, who for so long had felt like nothing more than additional chores for herself. Dojie was a bit of a problem, at a rebellious age, but still a sweetheart down deep. And Eukan, her son, she could just eat him up. This wasn't some weird idea, like that dreary *pünkscheit* superstition people still proposed. Her intentions were totally affectionate. He was a wonderful boy, and Sitund thought so too. They often lay together in the afterglow in bed, thinking about him, softly muttering, Eukan Severe, Eukan Severe; and their mouths would water, their palates throb, their eyes tear. He was their first son, their only son. How could they put it? He was so...so appetizing.

So now she gave six hours a week at the community stew house, where they served three hundred or more a day from a healthy pot of *cartnoct* riblets and *dreulasis* roots. This made her see how many people were down and hurting, people low on luck; and at the steam table she made a new friend, Thyka Abset, who dished out the millet and onions. She and Thyka volunteered together at the Monisantaca Shoe Riser, which was an expanding monument to the history of footwear, that put her in contact with a different kind of people, more artistic, interested

80

in artistic preservation. This Shoe Riser, or the Grand Heap of Shoes, was unique to Monisantaca, a monument to the kind of pedestrian citizenship first encouraged by Sorb Imulrèe, their greatest mayor. He was instrumental in setting aside space in the center of town for the Nealsty Burkick marketplace, now called the Kick. He had them build the stalls of the market around what was to become this Grand Heap, where everyone, whether a citizen of Monisantaca or not, was free to sign and leave his or her old shoes. During the forty years the Kick has been a successful marketplace the monument has been rising, its shape now like a huge hat, a knit fantasy with a brim. The lowest layer of the Heap was mostly brown or black, showing sensible shoes of the early period, times of conservative taste and frugality. It rose from there through a permissive period, expansive and relaxed, lacy networks of stiletto heels, and transparent pumps, then striations of garish colors, dulling into striations of mild pastels, followed by alternating stripes of white and red, until finally at the top the colorful sneakers of the recent era that looked from a distance like a merry tweed. Around the base of the heap, making up the brim, all the discarded sandals, zoris, and clogs gathered, to lend a surprising texture, like a conglomerated paper or bumpy weaving.

Yerml and Thyka received the shoes there for two hours every third day, and handed out elaborate receipts to people who wanted them for souvenirs. She also got to participate in the shaping of the monument, particularly now that young volunteers were so rare. She often climbed the Heap herself, up the heavy mesh that held it in shape, and placed the new contributions exactly where she wanted them. At first it was a struggle for her, but then as she got into better shape, she was more nimble and climbed like a fire-monkey. She loved having control

over the placement of new contributions, and loved to linger
up there at the top, from where she could see all of greater
Monisantaca, almost all the way down the Line to Slegeslona,
stretching between the Turb Scalranet, and the Blimclecledie
mountain ranges, and she could see Bysbu volcano standing
alone to the Northeast, if it wasn't covered in clouds. She could
even see Sitund's office window, and liked to imagine she saw
him looking at her from it, and would always wave to him before she descended.

This embarrassed Dojie deep into her afternoons, that
sometimes her mother was climbing on the Heap when she
and her friends were kicking. If she just glimpsed her mother
up there she got really embarrassed, afraid one of her friends
might say, "Hey, Dojie, there's your mom climbing up." It was
such a total gruel. She had to hide, try to steer her friends the
other way, even cover their eyes if they tried to look at the Heap.
That was deep snore anyway, so dumb. Who wanted to be reminded of all the stupid shoes? What was so great about walking, anyway? Footwear reaching to the sky? Muckworks galore.
Learn to skate some laterals!

Anyway, this was the day that her friend Lenoci Mindak
would be out for the first time, with her brand new ultimate
body puncture. She was due at the Kick for an exposé session,
to show it to all the brideys hanging out at the Trough. Lenoci
was so lucky to have parents who'd write a permission for her
to do it. Maybe it was because she didn't have a brother at all.
And she had a rich uncle who worshipped her and was willing
to pay for the whole thing. It was so double ultimate, so totally
drashy. Dojie ached to have this herself. She could feel it like a

squeezing on her spine. She could taste it in the whole middle of her body. They said it really hurt, but she had no doubt she could stand the pain, if she knew the result would be absolute drash. She always enjoyed the right kind of pain, anyway. She knew there was no way she could afford this, though. Faking the permission would not be a problem; but, as always, money was the big obstacle.

Only one person in the whole world really knew how to do this puncture, and he was willing to do it only for a lot of money. This was Dr. Deppster Johnjon, who lived right here in Monisantaca. He had given up a successful career in abdominal surgery to develop and focus on this puncture, which he told his friends allowed him to transcend the pedestrian world of surgery, into the raunchier realms of art. He was sick of being around the sick people, who only wanted to get better. Better was an illusion, he explained. He wanted healthy people around him to do something grand and cosmetic, make them feel the joy of aperture. His puncture was a total opening of the whole abdomen, from sternum to pelvis. The invention that put his genius on the map was the Deppster Johnjon Full-Body Grommet. He separated the internal organs to either side of the spine, so other people could see through the center of your body, really see daylight, or any kind of illumination for instance if it was night and you were at a party. Needless to say, it's a complicated and controversial procedure. Dr. Johnjon performs this with almost missionary zeal, right in the face of the commission that has him under investigation. For the people who want the procedure, it does a lot of good, he explains. Those who get it are changed profoundly, and those who don't are not affected. They remain the same. Dojie didn't care about any of the arguments, she just wanted herself to be opened up. She was ready as anyone for such a change in her life. But when would she ever have the money to do this? Up-front you had to pay for the grommet itself, which was a spinal casing and organ frame, recommended in gold, though a solid silver economy model was also available. Deppster Johnjon's great invention protected the spine. It had to remain straight. Curving it one way or another could cripple a puncture wannabe (though that might be drashy too, so empty and perverse.) The good young doctor designed this elegant casing for each individual's backbone, and the oval framework against which slimy organs, like liver, spleen, heart, intestines, and whatever else you've got, rested comfortably. The opening came out to look like an oval bisected vertically. It was a *phi*, looked like a *phi*. Of all the letters of all the alphabets she knew, she wanted to be the *phi*. It could be extra spanish, so drippy. The way all her brideys would look right through her. It would be the emptiest, drashier than grosbeaks. Dojie wanted to do this so bad. She had the guts. She had the backbone.

When she saw Lenoci displaying at the Trough, Dojie was very happy for her, but couldn't hold back her envy. Tons of brideys and their drones had come from everywhere to see her; even Eukan's gawks peered through the windows, so Lenoci finally had to raise herself up onto the ledge above the booth, to give everyone a good opportunity to look through her. It was the emptiest. It was the ultimate of drash.

"Dojie, hi," Lenoci greeted Dojie who pushed through the crowd, holding a *stormberry fragratto*. "I got those *phroa warmworms* you sent. They really helped. I've even got some left over, if you want them back."

"No, Lenoci. They're yours to keep. Use them up." She'd forgotten she'd sent them. One thing she really knew how to do was to get those *warmworms*; it was a talent she never even had to cultivate. She just often found that she was there, and there were the *phroa warmworms*. She supplied them for some of her friends, but only the most nickelish and flaunted, those she knew could handle them. She never sold them. That would be a whole other step, and in the wrong direction, she knew, in her young life. Selling *warmworms*, deep dangerous gruelmove.

"How does it feel," Dojie asked, as she slid into the booth, closer to Lenoci. "What's it like?" Dojie looked through Lenoci, to the shiny gold flecks of the formica wallboard. The spine was cased in gold from number four dorsal to number three lumbar, with an embossing of vines and apes climbing the whole length. "Well? What's it like, Lenoci?"

The punctured girl slid off the ledge, to sit down next to Dojie. "It's more ultimate than I ever imagined, Dojie. It's totally vacant."

"Does it hurt?"

"Still, just a little, but it's like sugar, like sweet pain."

"Oooh," Dojie moaned. "I know what you mean. I'm so jealous." The two friends kissed on the lips.

"You know my brother ran away?" Dojie said.

"Who?"

"Eukan. My brother. I was getting afraid for him with my mom and dad. They were starting to re-amorize, and they were coming at him with those words."

"Words? I don't understand what you're talking about." Lenoci had to strain her neck to see Dojie, because her body was wider now, and difficult to turn in the booth. Dojie liked that, thought it was really empty, to be almost two-dimensional. She could understand why Lenoci had some difficulty grasping what she said. In her new shape, she had a lot to figure out. Her friend switched to the other side of the booth, proudly fielding the gasps and exclamations of people gathered for a look-through.

"*Pünksheit* words," Dojie said.

"You believe in that stuff? *Pünkscheit* and stuff? I don't…"

As Lenoci leaned towards Dojie she grimaced. "Oooh… It still aches me a little, but it's everything so vast," she moaned. "I'll get used to it." She took a sip from Dojie's *fragratto*.

"Yeah, I believe in it. You just don't have a brother, so you don't have to deal. Ask Nonawi. She lost hers, and her parents are schoolteachers."

Lenoci's attention was elsewhere, partly distracted by the pain, and also because her boyfriend, Negger, was at the door. He never liked to come all the way into the Trough, because he was older. Most of the other kids didn't understand it, how she could go with someone so old, but Dojie did. Negger was really well displayed for an older drone, and young ones were such a snore, anyway.

"Hello, Dojie," he greeted her, smiling briefly, but ignoring all the other kids. "Lenoci, you have to come with me. I will get my motorcycle out of the shop. You will drive the car."

That was beyond drashy, Dojie thought. Lenoci didn't even have a license.

Lenoci stood up and kissed Negger in front of everyone. All over the Trough, even looking in through the windows, brideys and gawks craned their necks, to see what they could see through her—Negger's leather pants, his silver buckle. Everyone gasped in unison as he grabbed her spinal case, tipped her horizontal, her small breasts swinging out of her tube-top, and he carried her out like a valise, while she waved at everyone, spreading big thrills with her beauty-queen smile.

That was the grandest drash, Dojie thought. Possibilities were endless with such a supreme puncture. She wanted one so bad. It was out beyond the beyond.

By the time he woke up the fog was so thick, Eukan could hardly see where he was. He folded his silver blankets and looked for a trail, or any landscape feature, even a tree, but everywhere he looked in every direction everything looked the same, white upon white. He stood trembling in his quandariness. Tears filled his eyes. Why had he tried this at all? Dojie had convinced him, but he didn't need to listen to her. That was a lesson, if he ever got out of here. Even if he decided to go home, he would never find his way in the midst of all this cottony white. White was stupid. White was the color of fear. This was what he deserved for rebelling against his family, and a family he actually loved. He had a huggy mom who was a good mom, and a dad who was always there to teach him something. His dad would have taught him something right now, would have helped him get out of here. He called out, "Hello! Anybody. Dad!" but he knew the cry was futile. His voice flattened back against his face, going nowhere. This whiteness was as if overnight the whole world had been erased, and turned to cold. Was it a world? What kind of a place was this? Not a sound in it, except his own hiccups that had begun to at least reassure him that he himself was present.

Then suddenly he felt a whump, and another whump, so hard it felt like the ground trembled. Two whumps. His hiccups were history. All was silent again. He stared into the whiteness at the place where he thought the whump had hit. A friendly smell, like garlic roasting, came from there. In the middle of the smell he thought he saw a light, not exactly a light, however, but as if some of the fog had condensed and brightened. It was so cold. He draped a silver blanket over his shoulders. The light disappeared. He took a step towards where it had been, and it appeared again. Then it was gone again, until he stepped towards it again. That was it, like a follow-me from a storybook. He knew what he was supposed to do. The whiteness was fear, and the light was hope. He was supposed to follow the light, and so he did, up a hill, across a long flatness, and up again. The glow kept itself just in front of him, disappearing when he stopped and moving faster if he ran to overtake it.

He followed on a steep climb, with no trail that he could see underfoot, and huge boulders, big as his house, that he had to scramble around or climb over. "Wait a few seconds," he pleaded with the light. "I'm small. I can't go this fast." The light pulsed rapidly, impatiently, as it waited for the boy. "Where are you taking me?" he asked, and the light flew ahead. "Wait a second," Eukan told himself. "It's not taking me anywhere, I'm just following. Who told me to follow? Nobody. Why am I doing this?" Still nothing to see but fog, and a fine drizzle that soaked through his clothes. Eukan had to keep moving, to keep from shivering so much. That was why he moved, to forget how cold he was. He would never figure out how to get back ever again, wherever back was. It could be just a big circle he was moving in, like a joke played on him by this whatever it was. Who was laughing anywhere? Maybe nothing was there at all, just a figment. Then this fear grabbed hold, sank into his spirit. This wasn't real, this was a dream, and he was trapped inside, and he was tired, and he would never wake up. This was Hell, maybe his own special Hell, punishment for disobedience. He couldn't breathe. He had died; that was it, and this was Hell. But what had he done? What wrong had he done?

There was no one here to explain, no one to argue with. He had no choice but to follow this quirky light, just to keep going. Grandpa Hitchfred Alcock said, every time the old man took him on a hike, "Just put one foot in front of the other, one in front of the other. Then you'll get there." That's what he did. Forget everything else. One foot, then the other foot, then the one foot, then the other. He stopped thinking about what lay ahead beyond the next step, and then the next one, just put himself forward following the light, whatever that was. He felt like a foolish boy, a very tired boy.

He didn't notice at what point the fog started to thin, but he felt an arm of the sun slant onto his shoulders from around the curve of the cliff. Could this have been the sun he was following all along? Maybe yes, maybe not. And this was his first thought in a while about the Tanoke tree, and how would he ever find the elusive Sterub spider? He grabbed a few gasps of breath, and looked down. How high he was, and what a narrow ledge. His back pressed against the wall of cliff that leaned over him as if it would press him into the abyss, and he looked down at the thickness of fog below. It seemed too solid, as if he could step out onto it. He worked his way along this narrowing ledge into the full belly of the sun. Its heat swamped him, steamed the moisture out of his clothes. There, not three feet away, was the double-leafed top of a Tanoke tree, a huge one, its two enormous green leaves, dimly spotted with pink and violet, spread as if in welcome, the spore pod thrust from the center, ready to launch.

He could see that other trees in the tight little valley had already launched their pods, and dropped their leaves; and, in the distance, one launched right there in front of him, like a rocket thrust skyward, a sound like the tolling of a bell, the pod flying deep into the valley, leaves dropping. The exhilaration he felt at this sight was almost too much for his young body to sustain. He had to stop trembling. Then he felt another kind of fear, that he could be too late, that he'd better get to work on a tree before the pod launched, and that maybe he really didn't know enough about this to do it right. Maybe he was too young and too small. He took out his special heat blade, and held it in the sunlight till it was too hot to touch, then launched himself off the ledge, onto the leaf, and he slid down to where it joined the top of the tree. His flesh was green in the reflected light. He looked out into the valley, now totally free of fog, a whole valley of Tanoke trees. Who from Monisantaca had ever seen something like this? Who but the Etatreh peoples? He leaned back against the pod and started to cut. This could go any second. He felt the giddiness of someone finally getting to do what he always wanted to do. Within the leaf, he was cutting, and he was giggling. The cut went so slowly. He had to be careful and patient, to cut without gashing. He paused to heat the blade again. Soon there would be the Sterub spider to think about. Where would he ever find one? But forget it for now. Now he was cutting. He wished Ajieck were here to see him. He was Eukan Severe, and he was at the top of this Tanoke tree, and he was cutting leaf.

From his office window Sitund Monfahf could see the whole of the Nealsty Burkick marketplace, with the Bysbu volcano behind it in the clouds. He looked directly at the Monisantaca Shoe Riser, the Heap, where he occasionally saw his wife scrambling like a tiny monkey in the distance. How could that monument, which seemed so ridiculous in its conception, now be so moving? Sometimes he would sit and daydream at his desk, just looking at it, and he would feel all these emotions well up, tears in his eyes. Even before Yerml Perset volunteered to work on it, he had all these feelings. What was it? Just some shoes heaped up into the shape of a hat. But it hit him, it always swept something off the shelves of his heart. It was an emblem of loss, of all the people who had worn those shoes, many of them now gone forever. Now that he was having all these feelings for his sweet wife, his son, his family, he thought of all those families whose shoes rested forever in the Shoe Riser. He was so high and became so emotional that he had to pull the shade during meetings, for fear of suddenly breaking out in sobs.

It was a high. What kind of high? A contact high between himself and Yerml. It's a holding-hands-on-the-bus high. Like a high-school-crush high. A getting-home-before-the-kids high, jumping-into-bed high, sucking-and-licking high. A no-one-so-beautiful-no-one-so-sexy-as-you high, a no-one-so-hot-and-willing-as-you high. And it was a food high, for Sitund a cooking high. A run-to-the-store-for-the-raspberry-vinegar high. A French Purple Garlic high, none-other-will-do high. If he had it to do over again, he would work in that profession, making tasty stuff in his own kitchen; rather than what he did—working in product development for the manufacturers of plastic fasteners and films. Everything that was happening to him now, all this renewal of passion for Yerml, revisiting the elevations of their lust, feeling their subtle hearts open to each other again, holding each other every possible minute, sighing into each other, all this made him want to cook the greatest meal of all time. He wanted his whole family to be there, though Dojie these days was somewhat hopeless, seemed never to eat anything any more, had an attitude you couldn't split with a *stagnir* maul. But

Eukan was a different story. He and Yerml had such a passion for their son, feelings rich and deep. Their only son. He was so almost perfect. They owed him the best that life had to offer, and would give everything to help him grow in spirit, and fulfill his emotional and material potentials. Even if they would have to form something new of him, something great. Unlike his sister, he would not be a problem. Eukan would be happy to participate in a big way in this celebration. Eukan would be part of the feast.

Sitund had obtained months ago a special fat *yonoletenus* goose, and he had been nurturing and feeding it, a living goose. The prospect of a mouthful of the sweet, nutty texture of Yonoletenus breast made his mouth water. This was a rare treat at the table, because there were so few of these birds available at any time. They were difficult to raise, since they needed to graze on wooly *milfrion* grass. Each setting goose hatched only three or four goslings, and the gander or the goose herself quickly ate them as they pecked out of the shell. This was difficult to prevent because the goose would not sit on the eggs if there were the slightest hint of human meddling. You had to hope that the parents' hunger had abated by the second gosling or so, and then you could rush in and rescue one that was left. For this reason they were expensive, but it was worth it. Nothing could beat the fragrance and savoriness of *yonoletenus* meat, when it was cooked slowly in a glaze of cactus pear. That meant roasting it when *lacopani* berries were deep pink and ripe. Sitund fed these berries to the big gentle bird for three weeks before slaughter, 'til he could feel the bird full of juice. After hanging the carcass for thirty-six hours to let the meat change, he blew under the skin with a straw to separate skin from flesh, so the fat would drain and the skin crisp on roasting. He liked to stuff it with *treepflak* and roast it on a bed of its own feathers, which gave it a light pungency. For a sauce he prepared a purée of *arazazipp* beans that have been floated for several days in *lacopani* brandy. He would steam some vegetables, and make a nice dessert of frozen *lamar-spleam*. It was for Yerml Perset that he did this, because cooking for someone was always a sign of love, but also for Dojie, and especially for Eukan, their son.

"What a beautiful town we live in," he thought, as he gazed out his office window. "And the Shoe Riser, such a mysterious and beautiful monument to everyone. And what a great family I have. My heart is so full."

"Don't think you've looked at these yet," said his secretary, Lohly Uhrent, as she stepped into the office and placed some papers on his desk. She paused to smile at him. He didn't seem to notice. Over the last few weeks, his smile wasn't what it had once been for her. This was frustrating. They had lingered, until a month or so ago, on the cusp of an affair. She hadn't pushed it because this was strange for her, counter to her convictions. She had left her last job to escape the sexual advances of her boss. She would have battled it then, but she didn't like the job anyway, so she just quit. Though she had once vowed never to have an affair with a boss, nor with a married man, she found Sitund to be nice, gentle, self-effacing, a man with some power. She couldn't fool herself, she was attracted to him; so she decided to forego her convictions just this once. He was attracted to her as well, and that was why she let herself be so forward. "I think you should look this over," she said, leaning over his desk to expose her cleavage.

"Okay," he said, back still to her. He took some binoculars from a drawer and peered through them out the window, then waved at something out there in the distance.

She had found it to be fun. The anticipation of this flirtation got her out of the apartment and down to work happily on these mornings. Usually he enjoyed it as well. What could be preoccupying him now that was more important? She started to toy with him, just as a little test. "I've brought some talc, scented with hyacinth," she said, and then decided to become bolder, just to see if he was listening. "I'd be glad to powder your baubles."

"Good," his back still to her.

"And I brought a little petal-sneaker for your peezel."

"Okay. Okay," he waved his arm, back still towards her. "Leave them on the table."

She lifted her skirt, provocatively. "Shall I get undressed now?"

"Sure, yes, then just leave it on the desk, and I'll grab it when I go out."

"And if I come around there to kiss the little tickle-tail?"

"Don't worry about it."

He hadn't turned to look at her once. She could say anything, and he wouldn't get it. He raised the binoculars again, to look where? At that stupid Heap? Lohly dropped her hems. This was exasperating. She knew from talking to the woman she'd replaced that he'd had affairs with other women in the department, but unlike your average corporate sexual predator, who tried to take advantage of his clout, he was known to be shy, reluctant, though once the gates were opened, he was passionate and kind. That's how he was recommended. That was why she found him desirable. Lust in the office relaxed her more than a coffee break. So what was different about herself now, to make him ignore her? Something she was wearing? Her braces were invisible. She had recently broken up a long-term relationship that had stifled her, and although her mind frequently told her not to do this, her body would not let her quit. This still seemed like a decent alternative to just nothing—a light involvement with an attractive male, who was in no position to make demands on her. Except he was her boss, and that could turn into complications; but, so what? He wasn't the type to take advantage. He knew she could prosecute and win, if she had that inclination. It was a light dalliance. She was on her way out of this kind of work anyway. She studied fashion design at night. Lohly needed to nourish her artistic inclinations, to get out of this secretarial drudgery. She didn't want to be a boss, but she didn't want to be bossed any more, either. A little dalliance now was very attractive. Lust lite, with a married executive. There were worse things.

"You know, I think I finally understand it," he said, turning towards her at last.

"What do you understand, sir?" The *sir* she pronounced with an irony close to bitterness.

"My emotionality recently, so strong. Like why I'm so moved when I look at the Heap there. It's because it looks like a hat. Doesn't that sound stupid? It's made totally of shoes, but it looks like a hat. It suggests everything human by that. Between the hat and the shoes is the human being. Every human being lives between hat and shoe. That's what makes it so moving."

"Yes, sir," said Lohly, backing towards the door. She saw tears in his eyes. "Yes, sir. Hat and shoes."

"It makes me so happy to have this figured out. I often look at that heap, and feel these powerful emotions. I never understood that monument before. It's everything. It's human beings, a monument to all the peoples. And the way it exists across all the generations. It's the people now, the people historically.

Imagine the genius of Sorb Imulrèe, to make this possible for our generations, into the future. I'm so lucky to understand this now."

He was finally smiling at her, though it wasn't a smile for her, but something else. "Yes. Thank you. Glad you're happy." She backed out the door. Well, it wasn't what she had hoped. This was one of the crazier things that had happened, but she had to keep reminding herself that even without the affair, this was at least a job.

"Yes," said Sitund, a big smile on his face. "Yessss!" He sank down into his chair. "What is it about this day?" He relaxed into the satisfaction philosophers must feel when they arrive after long months of puzzlement at the answer to one big question. He lifted the binoculars again. Yerml was on the Heap, waving at him. She looked so appealing, balanced on top of that hat full of shoes. Balanced as if on all of humanity, man and womankind. He waved at her, though he doubted she could see him. He went to the window, and puckered onto the spot where he could see her tiny body as if it were wriggling on the glass.

Dojie sat on the low wall that surrounded the Heap, and dangled her feet in the shallow moat that circled it. Her mom had finally left, but not without first embarrassing her by coming over and fussing with her hair, some gruelly mother thing. She wished this progenetrice were more sensitive to what that looked like to her friends. She wasn't her mother's little girl any more. Something like that made her crave the body puncture more than ever. She never wanted to be like her mother ever. Lenoci's parents must have been a great pair of progs, but what did they think now that the puncture was totally on the screen, not just an idea? That's why Lenoci was drashy beyond commitment, to have gone through with the procedure. However, Dojie Resoft might as well forget about it. Not even ten years of the best summer jobs would let her afford the puncture. Not even if she sold her sex, like Ornash Sento; or like Gme Yran made porn flicks; or if she fed pictures of her body onto the World Wide Informator distriblastor, all of which alternatives disgusted her; but even if she did those things she would never make enough money in years for such a puncture. She had to do something else, something not so pricey, like ear removal, facial scrape, nose inversion, elbow locking, none of which had reached Monisantaca yet, which was so provincial, from Dojie's perspective. That was why kids here were spun in their own circles by Lenoci's drash. It would have been totally dry in Slegeslona.

She could find something to do that would cause her brideys to spin, something within her own price range, no problem. She and Nonawi Erryd had skiffed some ideas off the Informator, from this drashy nesting called Xupset Fron, which specialized in the widest of drash, busting all the moods. This was simple, but she could feel a whole world of drash supreme arising from it, no problem. This was permanent body tinting, derived from the practices of the ancient Etatreh peoples, whom she admired out-of-time. It would be going forward by going back. A big advantage was that this wasn't just a single revelation, like the body puncture, but you went through a whole sequence of transformations, like a golden yellow the first week, then royal blue, then green like eyes get, and a plump violet, and all kinds of other shades. And with a special wax technique you could make designs, which was beyond drashy, when you thought about everyone's tattoos. It would definitely jostle the progs, blow them off their snore stools. And her own brideys would pirouette around her, in and out of the Kick. Another great thing about it was that she could do it herself, there was no professional intervention involved, and maybe Nonawi could help. Then once she reached the deep teal she wanted to be forever, then she would bathe in the fixative, and that's the color you are for the rest of your life. No problem. It's real. It's a commitment. It's a "this is me" kind of a thing. She was going to do it. She had enough money now for the starter kit, that let you practice on a foot or a hand, and by the time she'd played with that and learned, she'd have enough saved for at least the whole-body primer tint.

"How's the wallow, Dojie?" Nonawi kicked some water onto her from the moat, then leaned over and brushed foreheads with her best friend.

"What?" Dojie was deep in her contemplation of the tinting.

"Nothing? Your brother? How is he?"

"Eukan?"

"Do you have another brother, that I don't know about?"

"I was thinking about something else. He's gone."

"O no," Nonawi said. "I'm so sorry. Dojie, that's horrible."

"No. Not that way. He's still somewhere." She waved towards the mountains. "Out there."

Nonawi looked in the direction she was waving. "I don't see him."

"Come on, None. He went to the mountains."

"Is he alright there?"

"I don't know. I guess so. He's real resourceful. I wasn't even thinking about him. I was thinking about something else."

Dojie wasn't ready to tell Nonawi yet. She wanted to try the sample before she fielded any opinions.

"So aren't they looking for him? Do the police know?"

"My progs can't tell the police. They're so obvious into their *pünksheit*. It's disgusting. The police would know right away what it was, and they'd throw Eukan into a protection unit somewhere."

"At least he'd be safe. That's better than being a meal for his progs. Why don't you tell the police?"

"Yeah, like they'd listen to me!"

Nonawi sat down next to Dojie, and dangled her feet in the water. They splashed at each other. Dojie imagined what it would look like if she had blue feet splashing. Ultimate. Beyond the beyond.

"When your brother gets back, I'm going to hug him 'til he squeaks."

"Eukan doesn't squeak," Dojie said, then they looked at each other and laughed like two girls.

With the evening chill, Eukan found the only way to reheat the blade was to hold it under his armpit, or once the sun had set, to fold it into his groin. Cutting the leaf was a longer job than anything he had read ever told him, and it made him sorry that he hadn't let Ajieck come with him. They could have taken turns. Every muscle in his body ached. He had no choice but to work through the night, through the pain, because he knew his tree was soon to launch its spore pod, and that would be it. "Don't launch yet, not yet. Please let me take your leaves first." Maybe it was crazy to talk to the tree, but this was his tree, and talking to it comforted him. The Etatrehs had talked to theirs.

He wasn't aware how long the night went on, but he kept working, and then it started to get light again, and just as the first bar of the sun flashed through a crease in the mountains he heard a sigh, and felt something release, and he hugged the trunk of the tree as both leaves wafted down. They floated as if they weighed no more than feathers. "You only float," he said to them, gripping the trunk with his arms and knees. "But I know how heavy you really are."

When he was halfway shinnied down the trunk he felt a convulsion, and then a wave, like a gulp that rolled up past his belly pressed against the tree, and he looked up to see the pod launch, take off into the wide skyline, and then he lost his grip altogether, and as he fell he thought he was done for, that was it for him; but almost as if it were waiting just for this to happen one of the leaves received him, and it was like falling into the mouth of a dream, and the leaf rolled with him inside, so this was no worse than falling out of bed, onto the carpet, not even waking up. And within this leaf, exhausted as he was, he fell asleep without hesitation.

He woke up several hours later, thinking about his mother, and how hungry he was. He would give anything for a taste of her land-prawn soup, and a ring-neck sandwich. He wiped tears from his cheeks. "Dad," he said. "What can I do now?" He just wanted to talk with his father a little, just a nice discussion like they sometimes had.

"Dad, soon I have to find a *Sterub* trundle spider. I've never seen one, except the small stuffed one at the natural history store in the Kick. A real one can be huge, the size of a giant church bell, the size of a school van. I don't even know if they're extinct. How do I find one, Dad?" Talking to a phantom of his dad only made him miserable. He crawled out of the leaf and stretched. He had to start his next chore, which was to connect the two leaves. He had read how to do it many times, but this was for real. Eukan muscled the leaves around so that knobs that were called the "buttons" on one edge of one leaf, lined up with the pores, or "buttonholes" on the other. It was not so easy to get them to join, or button up, as the books had made it seem. It took him late into the afternoon to get just a few done, and then to loosen the fan-like membranes that served as a rudder and propeller. He worked until dark, and into the night, and when it was nearly complete, he was too tired to admire it himself. He fell asleep again as the sun went down, knowing that when he woke up this time he would have to call out the *Sterub*, and that would be it.

It was another dawn when he awoke to thunder. Dark clouds tumbled over the mountains. He didn't want the boat to fill with water. Sometimes they spoiled, he'd read, when that happened before the trundle spider did its work. He began the long incantation that was supposed to summon this recalcitrant creature, a creature that was so huge, and yet ate nothing but the aphids off of dew-thistles. He sang this in a language he didn't understand himself, except for this peculiar translation of one of the quatrains:

> *O, spider, your day for me is here,*
> *And I grant you all my particular wow.*
> *This is the boat of my way to clear.*
> *I invoke you, appear and touch its bow.*

The rest was in the language of the Etatreh people. He chanted the whole incantation once, then chanted this again. He pressed himself against the trunk of a tree when the rain shower started. Was he supposed to go on chanting in the rain? Was he supposed to combine the chant with some kind of search? It seemed like empty hocus pocus, suddenly. Cutting leaf was one thing. It was an activity, at least. He was doing something. But this was unfamiliar magic. He kept the incantation going anyway, without listening to himself, as the shower ceased. "O, spider…" he went on. Suddenly, from around the exact place where he had been sitting before the rain started, something began to move. Then what sounded like an enormous yawn came out of the earth right there as a huge thing heaved itself up from the exact tuffet where he had been resting. Then a sigh came out, and he saw what was its identifying feature, its one humanlike eye. It stared directly at Eukan, and blinked. Another high-pitched sigh came out of it. "Yes, yes, yes!" Eukan filled with joy as the enormous thing turned and trundled over to his buttoned leaves, wheezing like an old bachelor who gets out of bed just before dawn to light the stove under the coffee pot.

She walked in the front door, glanced into the kitchen, and realized she'd better stay away. If a bomb had hit the kitchen, it couldn't have done more damage. As she was hanging her jacket in the hall closet, she heard a thud and turned to see a white cloud blow from the kitchen door. A bag of flour had probably hit the floor. When Sitund cooked he always bought it in forty-three pound bags. She didn't know how he did it. If she tried she couldn't scatter ingredients around the room and throughout the house as widely as he did. And he did this so lovingly.

The Noride nuts had been scattered clear across the living-room carpet, as if he didn't want anyone to miss them. She picked up a line of tiny, pricey Thwyneg Trowlap apples Sitund had laid down all the way from the kitchen to the bathroom, as if he needed this trace to find his way back from one to the other. She tasted one. It was like biting into a baby's eye, and it was sweet. As she stepped onto what looked like the field of battle, Sitund in his "Kiss Me I'm A Kitchen Slave" apron reached out for her and scattered the Trober beans across all the counters.

"Sweetheart, are you cooking or redecorating?" She swept some beans aside on the counter to lay down the tub of butter she'd retrieved from off the toilet tank.

"Shut up, beautiful, beautiful wife," he said. "I'm right in the middle of this." They kissed, and he sighed, feigning a melt to the floor. "I can't take it. You'll have to leave, or else I won't ever live to cook again."

"O, my goodness. The melodrama of my man in the kitchen."

"Shut up." He turned back to his mixing bowl. "I have to concentrate on this. I decided to do my Yonoletenus this way I never did it before. I always laid it on a bed of feathers. This time I'm making a crust, chopping the feathers and sticking them to a coating of ground Noride nuts in a purée of Trobet beans. The apples are for stuffing. If I get this just right when I crack it the feathers will separate from the crust, which I can halve into two tasty bowls for vegetables and stuffing. Edible bowls is a great idea." His grin, when he looked at her, made him look really stupid, she thought, but lovable. "So I have to mix it all now, and let it ripen in the refrigerator for three days."

"Then I can't touch you? I can't even kiss you right now? I can't grab your…"

"Shut up. No, I don't mean *shut up*, but please shut up. I just need quiet, to concentrate on this. The mixture reaches this critical consistency, and then you drizzle in the buttermilk as soon as the batter starts to dimple. So I have to…"

"After that you'll grab me, and tear off all my clothes, and ravage me across the carpet, through the spilled nuts and beans, and your fingers and your lips will…"

"Shut up…shut up, please!"

Yerml loved to see him so intense, and so domesticated. "We'll wait and see," she said.

"You won't be disappointed," sang her husband.

Yerml turned to see Dojie listening in the doorway, but she headed back upstairs, as soon as her mother looked her way. How much had she heard, Yerml wondered. And what difference did it make? She wasn't about to change things to protect her daughter. It finally had happened that after all this apathy, humdrum family life, tired old marriage, they were ready again to mush each other up every second. It was so rejuvenating. She wasn't going to change this, not even if it confused and embarrassed the kids. She was determined to keep it going, this husband and wife, transported by resurgence of passion. And they couldn't neglect their kids, not so much Dojie, who had this nasty teenage reaction to whatever they did, and they just had to put up with it, to wait her out; but Eukan, who was at that tender age, that stage of developmental succulence. They had to tend to him as carefully as Sitund watched the consistency of his batter.

"Dojie," she called from the bottom of the stairwell. She usually had to call at least three times to get a response. She took a couple of steps up. "Dooooojieee." No response yet. "Dojie, come down here a minute, please."

The door to Dojie's room cracked slightly, "What?" she whined.

"Come down here just a minute."

"Right now? I'm busy, mom."

"Right now, Dojie. When I say so. I'm your mother."

"Big and bushy, my female prog," she mumbled, as she patted her foot dry after the third soak.

"DOOQJJJIEEE!!!"

"I'm coming, mother," she shouted. "Bush-face," she mumbled.

Yerml was about to head upstairs and grab her, just as her daughter came bouncing down in her bra and bikini underpants.

"Is that the way you dress to come downstairs, young lady?"

"Duh, no mom. Of course not. I made a mistake."

"You know your father's home."

"O, he's cooking. And what's he going to see, anyway? My pubelets?"

"You should be more respectful, Dojie. And when you come downstairs you should always try to look decent. You never know who's here."

"I do look decent, Mom. Beyond decent. That's why you notice. You're jealous, Mom, of my beautiful body." As soon as she said that she wished she hadn't. She didn't know why she couldn't help being so cruel. Maybe it was the *pünkscheit* that made her weird too.

Her mother smiled. She'd heard worse from her daughter. This would all pass, she hoped. "I'm your mother, honey. You should show me a little respect, at least."

"Oh, Mom, sorry." Dojie lowered her eyes to look at her feet. She wished she was anywhere else. She wished she could grab hold of Shonirra Drof, her own older drone, and point his penis at her mother. That was a cruel thought too. Dojie wished she could go away. She couldn't, though, not while her brother was at risk.

Yerml followed her daughter's eyes down to her feet. One of them was yellow, up to the shin. "It's gone far enough already, Dojie. You have to tell us where your brother is hiding."

"He's not hiding."

"Then where is he? You know, and you're not telling us."

"Am I my brother's keeper," she sang, sarcastically.

Her mother sighed with exasperation. When she discussed her Dojie Problems with Thyka Abset, her friend at the Shoe Riser and community table, they always came to the same conclusion: that it was a stage that had to be tolerated, and that Dojie would get over this; but in the meanwhile, this was hard to get through day by day. "Why are you being so uncooperative? This is important." Yerml looked down and clenched her teeth in anticipation of her daughter's response.

"So important that you want to eat him, anyway," Dojie said, as she rubbed her hands together to warm them up. "That's all you want to do." She folded her arms across her chest, feeling a little chilled in her scant clothes.

"You don't really believe that. You don't know what you're talking about."

"*Pünkscheit!*" Dojie blew the word at her mother like an artillery round.

"I'm almost ready, sweetheart." Sitund leaned his head out the kitchen door, his face covered in a mask of powdered ingredients. "Hi, pretty kitten," he said to his daughter.

"Meow," she replied, maybe a little too sarcastically. She didn't want to feel this way about the progs, but they were different now. In their happiness between themselves the *pünkscheit* was fine, but for the kids, especially for Eukan, it was a disaster. "If you're so worried about Eukan, why don't you get the cops to search for him?" she asked her mother. Her mother sucked in a breath, and held it.

She covered her reddening face with her hands. "It's a family matter," she gasped. "It has nothing to do with the police."

The way of all progs, thought Dojie. "I'm cold. I'm going back upstairs,"

"What happened to your foot?" her mother asked.

"What foot?"

"That one. It's yellow."

"Oh," said Dojie, starting to climb the stairs. "I've got a yellow foot now."

The trundle spider stopped working each time Eukan attempted to look at what it was doing, so the youth had to feign sleep to keep the work going, 'til he eventually actually slept. The trundle worked through the night, and once it was done, a few minutes past dawn, it shook Eukan awake. He looked over, and couldn't believe it. A finished boat! "It's beautiful, thank you, Spider," he said. "It's so beautiful," he shouted to the spider again, to the forest, to the mountains, to the sky.

The spider then rose up on all its legs, and in one leap it landed on top of Eukan, and pressed him into the ground. "I'm not really a spider," he thought he heard the spider grumble, in a voice that was like big rocks rolling over each other. He lay there under it for a long time, pressed into the dirt. It wasn't heavy, but like a dream of weight pushing him down into the earth. He felt grains of dirt grind into his pores. He stayed there 'til he realized the spider, or whatever, wasn't going to move again, and he would have to crawl out from under. He did this with some difficulty, and slowly, because the creature, whatever it was, let out little cries of pain. Why would these slow movements hurt it. He was the one being crushed, who should be crying in pain. Finally he fought his way out, freed his body and stood up. When he looked back he saw what had originally been there, a large green mossy tuffet. There wasn't a trace of the Sterub left at all.

The boat was so beautiful, wide in the beam, and deep, symmetrical at bow and stern. The spider, or whatever it was, had sealed the central seam perfectly, and its narrow keel was penetrated at intervals, for when he wanted to bolt a wider keel onto it, for his journey into the rougher deeps. The gunwales were a hardened extrusion of the trundle's silk, that stretched and curved the sides of the boat, widening some pores through which he could later thrust the oars. There was a convenient notch at the stern, to which he could attach a biological motor should he find a propellor plant. And he had to fashion a rudder, and fix that in place too. Now that it was over with, everything seemed to have been so easy. He forgot about the terror he'd felt getting there, the thoughts that he might be lost forever, and the dangers of cutting the leaf. That's all he'd really done, he thought, was cut the leaves, and then button them together. Whatever it was, what he'd known as Sterub trundle spider, had done the rest. Now he had this wonderful boat, thanks to those Etatreh peoples who first developed the way to make this, and originally trained the spider to do this work. All Eukan had left to do was to get the boat safely into the water.

By his estimation, the river was about two hundred and fifty feet away. He had hoped the spider would have stuck around long enough to help him launch his craft. He loved calling something his "craft." How could he move so much weight by himself? He was just fifteen years old, and of average size, and he knew the limits of his own strength. If his dad were here to help him, he would think nothing of it. Even Dojie could be a help, though she'd complain all the time. And Ajieck, of course. But this was his own problem, and so far he had worked it out alone, and now had to finish alone. The *pünkscheit* progs, as Dojie called them, were his own problem, even though his sister worried about it a lot. He had to face it himself. No one else he knew, not even Ajieck, had expressed interest in building this boat. This was his project, win or lose; his to solve, his to surrender. He rubbed his hands together the way he saw his father do it when he was about to get down to work. He saw a corridor clear to the river, if he moved some branches, and trimmed a little. And he could roll it, probably on some of the logs fallen hereabouts, but would have to trim and debark them too to make them smooth for rolling. He went down the bank to the river, which was just a large brook at this point. It seemed deep enough to float his "craft." Wait 'til he showed it to Ajieck and the rest of his gawks. He started working, and felt an elation he had never felt before. A great energy of joy embraced him, and he popped a boner as he worked, and couldn't explain it, and was glad he didn't have to. All day he labored at clearing the track, and trimming rollers. There was no way this wouldn't work. None of his gawks had ever done something like this. "Thank you, Etatreh people," he stopped to say occasionally, then dipped into the brook and splashed the sweat off himself, and ate the little Clickfish he caught sucking on his fingers. Exposure to air cooked and crisped them instantly.

To expand the barbecue pit, Sitund had to work during the day, when his neighbor wasn't home. He lined it with stones taken off the wall that separated his yard from the yard of Borter Lalvud, with whom he'd had his differences. The neighbor claimed this fence was one hundred percent on his side of the line. Sitund said it split the line. The original barbeque pit was big enough for a Yonoletenus goose, but not for whatever else they were going to roast on the spit at this coming family celebration. He extended it in each direction, a shallow pit, lined with flat stones, that he would soon cover with charcoal. At one end it was a little deeper, where he would bury the goose in its tasty jacket, but the rest was exactly the right depth, over which a spit could turn slowly, something special on it, fat rendering onto the glowing coals in pops of blue flame.

He had to shop for charcoal, paper plates, salad fixings, beer and assorted soft drinks, and wanted to get that done this afternoon. In the house Dojie moved around her window, half-dressed or half-naked, depending on how you looked at her. Eukan still hadn't shown up from wherever he had gone. The picnic was mostly for the son; in fact, without him it would be an empty ritual. He was confident Eukan would be back in time. He had raised a responsible boy. However he wasn't so confident his wife would get back with the van in time for him to shop for a new picnic table, the old one an embarrassment, rotten and collapsed. Part of Yerml's sweetness was that she was so vague, and it didn't really register with her that he might need the van. She seemed oblivious to the fact that stores would close, days could end, people had deadlines, and even that someone might really want her help and support.

It was five forty in the afternoon when he finally heard the van pull up, the door slam, and there in the entryway was his

Yerml. O heaven in the flesh! Yerml, his Yerml. Her look melted him, and when they embraced, all their ingredients mingled.

"You got back just in time. I hope I can get everything done."

"I said I'd be back. What did you expect?"

"Nothing, sweetheart. I want everything to be perfect." He took the van keys from her hand.

"We trust you. Don't worry. Mr. Pillar-of-Strength." She looked into the kitchen, and the living room. "Is he upstairs?"

"No. Not home yet."

"It won't be a picnic without him."

"I dug a new pit. He'll be here. I'm going for a new picnic table. He's a satisfier, our son." He and his wife melted into each other again. "Yum," they said in unison.

Eukan had actually returned. He had climbed through a basement window and had slipped undetected up to his sister's room, and was helping her tint her foot green, as he told her, in excited bursts, the story of his boat, his trip down the river.

"...like the boat did most of it by itself...a pair of propellor plants for a small biomotor...didn't even have to stimulate it...a rudder but it steered itself...awesome fast boat...should have seen Ajieck and those gawks...your brother built it...me... glides like a cloud on the wind...you have to see it, Dojie..."

"Okay. I'll come see it, but first you've got to hold the foot really still, Euk, or else you're no help." She was applying the special wax in a star design, to practice this masking, so a yellow star would shine through. She wanted to get really good at this, so when she did the final teal she could make an elaborate something all over her body. What could it be? A big dragon, maybe? Something drashy beyond drash. Maybe a dramatic tortoise on skates. She would do something to send the empty beyond.

"It went so easy on the top of the shallowest rapids…spun around and around but never even wobbled…I love my boat …I love my boat…"

"Hold it like this," she twisted her foot, "and don't let it move."

Eukan gripped her foot. She was his sister, and he loved her a lot; but sometimes he couldn't figure out why she did what she did. "And it's like my boat steered by itself all the way down here. It came right down here. I didn't have to do anything."

"Well bugbug, Eukan. The river only goes one way, from there to here. Besides, you've got to get away from here soon. A good thing you've got that boat."

"Dojie, why are you making your foot green?"

"Dojie," they heard their mother call, as she started up the stairs. Eukan dove into the closet. "Dojie!" Her mother threw open the door. "Why don't you ever answer me?" She looked around the room.

"I answer you."

"You should answer right away." She looked down at Dojie's foot, and wrinkled her nose. "You'll clean up your room, and help me straighten up downstairs. Picnic's tomorrow. Big barbecue, sweetheart." She pointed at the foot. "Looks like a disease."

"A barbecue, huh?"

"If your brother ever gets back. It'll be pointless without him."

"Brother, yum yum," she said, sarcastically. "Sadder if he comes. Is he a missing person yet?"

"After tomorrow we'll worry about that, if he doesn't show up. Now we have sheets and a tablecloth to iron. Pillowcases."

She reached out to open the closet where Eukan was hiding. Dojie pushed her hand away, and stepped in front of the door.

"What are you doing? That's my closet."

"You're living in this house, young lady, and not paying rent..."

"What do you want? It's my closet."

"I was just going to grab some of your old sneakers and take them to the Heap."

"The stupid Heap. I'll bring them down later, okay. Stay out of my closet."

Yerml almost shoved her aside, as an object lesson. She was still nothing but a kid, as long as she was a dependent. Her closet. Really? What did she keep in there? Some time she'd come up when Dojie wasn't home and go through the mess herself, but she'd let it pass for now. These were the joys of motherhood, indeed. People who believe that should try it some time with teenagers. "So come down and help with the ironing."

"I don't do ironing." Dojie said that to be nasty. She didn't like herself nasty, but her mother sometimes was so clueless and bossy.

"Okay, but you can at least help me with the wash." Yerml would be grateful for any small victory.

Dojie lifted her green foot, as if to flaunt it. Her mother wrinkled her nose. "I don't know why you want to do these things to yourself," Yerml said.

"I want to walk on a foot of a different color," Dojie said, self-righteously, and then she laughed at herself.

"Well, you've sure got one now." Her mother laughed too. Sometimes she almost seemed to understand. She'd been a bridey herself at one time, though they didn't call themselves that, back in the old times.

Eukan slipped out of the closet, as soon as he heard his mother go back downstairs.

"It's time you'd better leave," Dojie whispered. "You heard what she was saying. You've got to get away from here."

Eukan rubbed his hands down his cheeks. "Not yet. I can't yet. I have to figure everything out first."

"What do you have to figure out? You heard her say barbecue. Do I have to convince you again about *pünkscheit*? It is coming."

"No. Yes. I can't think about it." Eukan laughed nervously.

"It's not a joke."

"I don't think it's a joke. It just doesn't seem possible. It seems so stupid. Mom and Dad can't be that stupid."

"How long's it been since we've had a barbecue? Pure and simple *pünkscheit* is what they're into. Nonawi's family did him in midwinter, and they had a big boil. Yuk, boiled brother. Turned Verri into, like, a lobster. They feasted on him, a couple of cannibals. And they're schoolteachers. So much for education. It sounds too silly to talk about, but this is real, and it's horrible."

"You'd like barbecued brother better, anyway. Right?"

Dojie screwed up her face in exasperation. Even though he knew this was happening, Eukan couldn't take it seriously while he was in his own home. He'd always felt secure here.

"At least I got to build my boat."

"Eukan, look straight into this. It's not about building a boat. It's not a hobby. It's keeping you alive so I can have a brother. You can't be just some meal for the progs. I don't want to have to look at them and say, 'There's my brother, in their bellies.'"

"You shouldn't call them progs."

"You'd better leave now." She stomped her green foot for emphasis.

"I'm already gone, Dojie. But first I've got to get some of my things organized, figure out what I want to take, tell all my gawks goodbye. I can't just leave, like leave. In a couple of days I'll be ready."

He was the most gruelly brother, far beyond exasperation. "And in the meanwhile you're going to stay in the house?"

"I guess so."

"Sleep here? In your own room? Don't do it."

"Yes. I will." Her objection made him more stubborn.

"They'll find you for sure. Then you'll be toast, I mean worse than burnt. Eukan, you are such a gruel."

"Why do you use those weird words? Prog? Gruel?"

"You call them your gawks. What kind of word is that?"

"That's what they are. What's a gruel?"

"You!"

No one had to convince Ajieck to stay with the boat. It was love, immediately, first-sight. He would have been there even if Eukan hadn't asked him. He was so in awe of his friend, his primary gawk, who had built this, had made the trek into the mountains, and come back with a boat. Eukan was definitely the most elevated of all the gawks in Monisantaca, in their circle or in any other. Ajieck saw the boat and knew immediately that this was where he was going to stay forever. Live in this boat. Make his home in this boat. Heaven is this boat. He packed everything of his own he could take away from Ronyalmy's house. She was his foster mother, and she was okay, but she was getting older

STEVE KATZ

and would be relieved he was gone anyway. She'd do better with another kid, perhaps a bridey, because girls are preferable. He and Eukan could leave Monisantaca altogether, leave all the parents, and all the circles of gawks, and all the schoolteachers and coaches and his music tutor, whom he loved; but so what! He'd take his trombone. It would be so great to practice as they floated down the river. Eukan would have his mandolin. It was a little scary, but they were both ready to leave, Eukan to escape the *pünkscheit*, Ajieck just to leave and find out what his own life was going to be. Mandolin-trombone duets all the way to Slegeslona and beyond.

As soon as he woke up, and washed his face in the river, and ate a few of the biscuits Ronyalmy had packed for him, he took his trombone out of its case, put a mute in the bell, and sat down on the stool she had let him take from the house. It gave him a little twinge to think of how nice his foster mom was, and how these biscuits were to be the taste of his final separation from her. He played a few long blue notes in honor of Ronyalmy, of Monisantaca, of all his gawks, though not Eukan who was on his side of the blues, but of all the teachers, of his kayaking coach, of everything he was soon going to leave behind.

It was those long muted trombone notes that Eukan was shocked to hear as he approached the boat in the morning. He saw the tarp stretched over the stern, and couldn't believe Ajieck had let this happen. Someone was in the boat. When he looked over the gunwale he was even more disturbed to see it was Ajieck himself. He had trusted his friend just to guard it; but here he was taking up all the space, his stuff piled up like junk under the tarp in the stern.

"Ajieck! What's going on? What's all this stuff doing here?"

"It's all that we'll need."

"It's my boat, Ajieck. I made this boat." Something had been violated, he felt. When he brought it down the river it had been so pristinely his and now someone had filled this most private secret sacred space with alien stuff. "This is my boat, Ajieck."

"It's just...If we leave, I thought...We can use all this..."

"When did I say you could come with me?"

"We always talk about it, how we were leaving together, how we were going to go, what we were going to eat. Now why are you being stupid? I thought this time..."

"It's my boat. Who asked you to stuff it up like this? I don't know where I'll end up. I'm the one who has to get out of here. It'll be dangerous, and weird. You don't know how weird it's already been."

"So? That's even more why I have to come. You can't do this without me."

"I can. I already built my boat. I already got this far."

"This far is only where you started from."

"So what? It wasn't easy. I did it myself. You didn't even see what I had to do."

"You could have done it better if I was there."

Eukan clenched his fists. "What could be better than this boat? You can't come. What makes you think you can come?"

"I'm coming. I already left."

"You can't come."

"I'm coming. I said goodbye to Ronyalmy already. She gave me this stool."

"You can't."

"I am."

"Yak yak yak yak yak," mocked Dojie, looking down from over the gunwale. Nonawi peeked her head over too. Ajieck sat back down with his trombone, and blew some spit out the spit valve.

"Wow, look at this," said Nonawi, jumping into the boat. "It's so big."

"My brother, Eukan, built this," Dojie said, proudly, as she followed her friend into the boat. "By himself, alone."

"And all this good stuff you've got to take with you," Nonawi said, looking at Ajieck's possessions piled neatly under the tarp.

"It's just stuff," Eukan said, grumpily. "I don't need any stuff. And I don't need someone else in my boat."

Nonawi stepped closer to him, and put a hand on his head. She was several inches taller than he. "What do you mean? I see a sleeping bag, a shovel, what must be a tent. There's a box of food. You'll need everything when you go." She looked at Dojie, then pulled Eukan against her body. "I told you I just wanted to squeeze him," she said to Dojie.

"Fumm nopf fing nywhff," said Eukan, as she held his face pressed into her breasts.

"What?" Nonawi pushed him away, to arm's length. "What did you say, sweety?"

"I'm not going to go anywhere."

Ajieck, who was softly imitating the sounds of their conversation on his trombone, blew a dramatic low note at this last statement.

"Eukan!" Dojie was alarmed. "When did you decide this, now? You can't *not* go. That's crazy. Tell him, Nonawi."

"That's crazy," she said.

"Tell him more."

"Your whole life is in danger." She tried to hold him again, but he pushed away. "Your whole future." Nonawi wiped some tears from her eyes.

The boy grouched around, looking at Ajieck, who continued calmly playing notes. Eukan hit the slide of the trombone with his knee, and grunted aggressively.

"Tell him more. Tell him what happened to your brother," Dojie insisted.

"I can't tell that. I don't ever want to think about it again."

Ajieck played a long C-sharp, and Eukan smacked the bell of his trombone with the back of his hand. "I won't go anywhere. I don't care. I live here."

"You can't mean that. You can't live here, and live, Eukan."

"I don't care."

"Tell him, Nonawi."

Nonawi sank to her haunches, back pressed against the side of the boat. "Okay. I'm going to tell you about this. It's a horrible story, and I never tried to tell anyone before. If I even think about it I'm crazy for weeks. But I have to help you, Eukan. I don't want Dojie to lose her brother like I lost mine. This is what happened to my brother. Do you remember Verri Hoxnepi? My big brother? You don't, do you?"

"No," Eukan mumbled.

"You know what happened to him, don't you?"

Eukan covered his mouth with his hand. "Only what Dojie told me."

"I told him what I knew." Dojie shrugged.

Nonawi lowered her eyes, and pulled in a deep breath. "I don't think I can."

"Please, tell him," Dojie said.

Eukan moved closer to her, and Ajieck blew air through his horn. "Tell me what happened to him. Please," Eukan said, softly, as Ajieck started to climb the B minor scale.

"He was my big brother," Nonawi began. "And I was only twelve, and I didn't know about the *pünkscheit*, the way Dojie does; otherwise, I would have helped him." She paused and sighed.

"Now you've got little Ralck Agelb, and he's a cute little drone, very handsome, I'm told," Dojie tried to reassure Nonawi.

"I don't...I can't even look at him; I mean, I should. He's my little brother; but it's like I know why he's here and I miss Verri Hoxnepi so much. I don't even want to see any Ralck, even if he's a perfect kid. I can't..."

She stopped again to still her sobs, and they listened to Ajieck slowly step down the B minor again. Then she went on. "Late that night I woke up. I thought it was because the ticking of the clock my mom had just put in our room was so loud, and I looked at the clock, then I saw my mom and dad kissing by Verri's bed. They kept kissing forever, and when they finally separated I saw Verri lying on the bed, on top of his blankets. He was all naked." She sobbed, and grabbed the slide of the trombone, as for support.

"Right then I knew something was wrong, but I didn't dare make a noise. I remember the time. The clock said it was three thirty-three when they picked my brother up, his whole body. I don't know if he was dead yet, or what, but they carried him out of the room. I waited a moment, and then I followed them. As they carried him down the stairs they were singing a song, like 'Where Have All the Flowers Gone.' I hate that song. I followed and they hauled him into the kitchen, where a huge pot of salted water was boiling, like I'd never seen a pot that big before, and it took up the whole surface of the stove, all the burners. They laid my brother out on the counter, and his arm and leg slipped off and he almost flopped to the floor, but they caught him. I couldn't see if he was breathing or anything. I hope he wasn't. I hope he was dead already, and couldn't hear my dad sharpen the carving knife, *swiip swiip swiip*, and then I hope he couldn't feel anything when my dad cut through his belly. The guts slopped into a bucket my mother was holding. I don't know, but he looked at me. Maybe I imagined it, but I remember he smiled. I still see that smile." Nonawi paused to wipe some tears from her eyes. "Do you want to hear the rest of this?" she asked Eukan. Eukan grinned meekly, and shrugged.

"Did you watch the rest of it?" Ajieck asked, putting down his horn.

"I saw all of it," Nonawi said.

Dojie sank to her haunches, and held her hair wrapped around her face.

"Then you should tell it," Ajieck said.

Nonawi looked at Ajieck as if he was a hostile stranger, then she continued. "It was so messy, so much stuff inside my brother, and blood, and Dad kept cutting and Mom kept cleaning up, except when they stopped to kiss again. They kissed plenty, their faces all bloody, and I watched it all. They had him down to a carcass, with the skin still on. He seemed so small just as a carcass. 'That's good enough,' mom said, and they stepped back from the job they did, leaned against each other, and held hands. 'Thank you Verri Hoxnepi,' they said. 'You are a good son.' Then they folded my brother up, and dropped him into the boiling pot. I remember the first rays of morning stabbing me through the kitchen window, through the steam that rose from the water that had splashed to the floor, and I remember his hair, a long braid of hair, hanging over the rim of the pot."

"He was so much the emptiest drone," Dojie sobbed. "He was drash beyond drash beyond the beyond." She was crying. "Yes, he was, Dojie. He really was, wasn't he? You should have known him, Eukan. So what I did was when my progs went outside, and they were doing that morning sun thing they still do, I went down to the pot, and cut off Verri's braid, and took it back to bed with me, and wrapped myself all around it, thinking maybe I could bring my brother back with just my own little body. That braid is all I have left of him. Still I sometimes comb it out and braid it again. It's all I have." She paused and looked around. No one was looking at her. Dojie had pulled Eukan down to herself, and was trying to hug him. Ajieck sat on his stool, his trombone at his feet, his fingers tapping on the bell. "That's about it," Nonawi said. "I never told this before. It's weird to tell it. It feels different."

"Did you ever eat any?" Ajieck asked.

She screwed up her face at him again as if he were some kind of alien antagonist, but she answered. "I couldn't have. Progs don't offer that meat to the sister, but I could never, anyway. Who could? Oh, yes, about a week after they sogged him I came home early for lunch. Both progs were still at school, teaching. I went into the garage, and there was Verri Hoxnepi's head propped on a rotating plant stand my mom had once used for winter narcissus. It was almost nothing but skull. They had eaten the lips and cheeks. They were waiting for the brain to ferment. It was streaked with black, teeth all yellowed and gross. It didn't even look like Verri, but who else would it be? Anyway, I pulled up a chair and sat down there, spinning the top of the plant stand slowly, and just looking at Verri Hoxnepi. I sat there for hours, 'til I heard my mom's car. I didn't say a word to him, because I knew he couldn't ever answer me again. Before I left him in the garage I kissed him goodbye, his yellow teeth."

"You kissed a skull, kissed it?" Dojie wrinkled up her face.

"That was my brother's. What would you do? I'd never see him again."

"You could have walked away. You didn't need to look at that," Ajieck shouted. While everyone was listening to Nonawi, he had untied the boat at the bow so it flagged out into the river, and then he had pulled out his antique bayonet from his stash and had run balanced along the gunwale and stood on the stern with his machete raised, ready to cut the boat totally loose. "Since when is there a law somewhere that you have to watch? It was your choice. You could have turned your back, gone somewhere else. It's because there's no place crazier than here. We should burn the whole place down. You're not a grownup. You didn't have to watch that nasty stuff."

Dojie had bunched herself up into a ball of sobs, rocking in the middle of the boat.

"What are you doing, Ajieck?" Eukan suddenly roused himself from the tragic reverie. "Don't cut it. Don't cut that."

"We're all gonna go. We can't stay here. We're all going." Ajieck lifted the machete above his head.

"Ajieck, drop that thing. This is my boat. If you cut that rope, it's mutiny. And you're not my friend after that."

"We're not...we can't be...we're leaving." He brought the machete down in a broad slash against the rope, but the edge was too dull, and the bayonet sprang back up, almost tossing Ajieck into the water. He knelt down then and sawed across the rope, trying to sever it thread by thread.

Eukan picked up Ajieck's trombone, and held it over the water. "If you cut any more, I'm dropping this into the river.

Say goodbye to your happy 'bone."

At first Dojie thought, after hearing the story, it wouldn't be so bad to leave right then. Everything about Monisantaca seemed calamity and horror. Then she remembered she hadn't finished her body tinting, and she didn't want to leave anywhere till she proved to herself she would do it, till she finished enough to display herself for all of her brideys.

When she spotted Lenoci and Negger strolling along the wharf she immediately coiled up the bow rope and called out to them. "Catch this, Lenoci, Negger. We're drifting." Negger immediately released Lenoci, and caught the rope in his big right hand, and pulled the bow into the wharf. The dispute between Eukan and Ajieck seemed to end when they both saw Lenoci. Neither of them had ever had the thought that anyone could be so thoroughly punctured. It was as if such a miracle could be a balm against conflict.

"Is that your friend?" Eukan asked, waving the trombone at her. Nonawi, then Dojie, climbed out of the boat. Ajieck grabbed his trombone.

"Why did she do that to herself?" Ajieck asked, as the two girls ran over to greet their friends.

Dojie turned back to look at her brother and his friend. They suddenly seemed very young to her in that big boat. "Gruel number one," she said, pointing at her brother. "And gruel number two." She turned back to her friends, and they all walked away.

Everything he had once called home was suddenly strange to Eukan, his room and all his stuff, as if nothing could be his any more, nothing belonged to him any more, not even the precious baffler coat his father had given him on his four-teenth birthday, not even the *Tighovnoj* trilogy that he had want-ed so badly to read again. The Kerpar Yespo suction sandals, that would be so useful in a boat, seemed to belong on other feet than his. The heavy sweater he'd inherited from his sister, that even shed water, seemed an artifact from someone else's life. Everything from his past had been drained of himself, and he felt this hollowness at the core of his being. He attributed his deep disorientation to the fact that he had decided to go against his parents' wishes. But he had a right, an obligation to save his own life. He thought that, but then he thought that maybe this was the wrong thing to do, maybe he should stick around to see what *pünkscheit* was all about. How could it be so bad? He had always loved his parents, and was not like some of the gawks he knew, who threw up when you mentioned a mom and a dad. But Nonawi's story of her brother's head turning on a plant stand was too powerful a warning. Winter narcissus? He didn't even know what that looked like. Life is bizarre; at least, that's what he was finding out. He couldn't imagine his mom and dad barbecuing his body, or anything like that. If it wasn't for Dojie he would probably stick around, even if it was true, and he knew they did intend to make him into meals. How weird that sounded. He was their one son. He was only young. How could they do this? He couldn't go against their wishes now, when he'd always been so obedient. What was life worth if he had to abandon his mom and his dad? He didn't want to oppose the will of his father, disappoint his mother? So many other boys had faced their fate, why shouldn't he? Some had even survived. He wanted to live the rest of his life. His mom and dad loved each other. They loved him too. He was sure of that. Abraham loved Jacob. He was sure of that too.

All this stuff, he thought, as he packed his duffle. *All this stuff doesn't belong to the person who will carry it away. Without the parents none of it would even be here, and neither would I.* He looked in the mirror. "Who are you?" he asked, but he got no reply, nothing to encourage him to do this, nor to discourage him from doing that.

Very early in the morning, Sitund emptied the last of twelve bags of charcoal into the freshly dug pit, and sprayed it all with charcoal starter. Yerml, who was watching from the doorway, crossed the yard to take his hand. It felt sweet, to lean against each other. "We'll light it now," Sitund said. "And keep it burning through tomorrow so we're sure all the bitter fumes are seared out of the freshly dug roots, and it'll seal the ground underneath, and then everything will be ready for the goose, and for whatever else attends our barbecue."

They both looked up at the window of Eukan's room. "Did you see that?" Yerml asked, agitated.

"What? That?" He pointed at the window.

"Yes." They'd both seen a shadow cross the shade pulled down over Eukan's window. "He's home."

They turned to each other and embraced, kissing deeply. "He's home," they said in unison. "He's a good boy."

"I hope you got some crispy *puffducks*," Yerml said. "I want Dojie to enjoy herself, and she always can eat a roasted *puffduck*, even now, though she's such a fussy one about food."

"Good idea. I'll go get some." Sitund looked up to Eukan's window again. His heart yearned for his son. "Perfect boy."

"He will be perfect, by-and-by. Perfecter and perfecter," cooed Yerml.

Sitund and Yerml aimed at perfection. That was their goal as parents.

That afternoon, Sitund added more charcoal and raked the coals across the pit. He liked to get an even glow overall, though it was pleasing to see the intensity vary as a light breeze played across. He looked up at the fence around his yard and saw his son dragging a duffel, trying to hide behind the sparse shrubbery. Sitund ran around to confront his boy at the gate.

"Eukan, where have you been?" asked Sitund, in a pleasant tone.

"I've been to the mountains," said Eukan, staring at the ground.

"Alone, my son? To the mountains?"

"Alone, sir. I was alone as I went there," Eukan said, and then mumbled, "and here I am alone as well."

Sitund gripped the boy's thin arm with his big hand, and pulled him into the yard, towards the barbecue pit. "My son, you are still a child. You must not do something like that without permission, without our supervision and advice."

"I am sorry sir; but I had no choice." Eukan felt his father's grip. The pain was a revelation, pressing down to the bone. His father dragged him closer to the pit. They made him feel confused and desperate. "What have you done here, sir? For whom are you burning these coals?"

"This is our barbecue pit, my son." The coals sparked and reddened, though no wind had crossed the surface. A wave of heat engulfed them.

"Father," the boy shouted, so loud that he startled Sitund who lost his grip on the arm. Eukan sprang back. His son had never addressed him so formally before, had called him "dad" and "pop" and even "sir," but never "father," and never so loud.

"Father," the boy brayed. A wave of confusion crossed from son to father, a premonition of remorse. He reached out for the arm again.

Eukan jumped back. "Father, what do you roast in this barbecue pit?"

"We will..." His father lunged at him again, and missed. His voice faltered. "To...mmmorrow we will see...n...n... nnothing today."

"Eukan," Dojie shouted, as she stepped from the kitchen door, then she bounded into the yard, wearing only her bikini underpants. Sitund gazed at his daughter, and was amazed. This was his daughter, and she was a woman. She had finished the teal tint on her legs, and had figured a design of orange flowers on a pale green vine, starting from her ankles, and opening onto her thighs. She found she had a talent for this, and it was going faster even than she had hoped it would. In her mind she had a picture of the animals she wanted up her back, and across her breasts. She would need help for that.

"You should cover yourself, daughter," said Sitund, staring at her. "What have you done to your legs?"

"My legs?" she said, happy to see that she'd distracted her father long enough for Eukan to run back to the gate, grab his duffel, and disappear. "I don't understand. What about my legs?"

"Your legs have that peculiar color on them."

"Well, Father. That is my color from now on."

Her father noticed suddenly that Eukan was gone, and he looked to the gate, and took a few steps as if to go out himself. "Eukan," he called, "son." Then he gave up. "Oh, well. He'll be back," Sitund said.

"I'm afraid he will," Dojie said, and she looked into her

father's face, into his eyes, and for the first time saw the sadness and confusion there.

On the following morning, when the queer pale tints of dawn raised their green veils from the western horizon and in all the tallest *Mediroome* trees the *Crubeliwlis* birds awoke to sound their yawning songs, Sitund and Yerml stole from their beds and crept through the hallway to their son's bedroom. Sitund concealed behind his back a net knotted of the strongest sisal hemp, reinforced with a finely drawn steel filament. Yerml held another end of the net with two small fingers of her left hand. She turned the knob carefully on Eukan's door, and pushed. The hinges squeaked as the door swung slowly open, and a body stirred in its bed, under the thin blanket. They paused, and listened to their son's breath, as it deepened again. They kissed lightly on the lips. "Regular, deep respiration. Nice," said his mother, and they stopped at the foot of the bed. They paused again to synchronize their breathing with their son's. Yerml carefully rolled back the blanket. Eukan wore the pajamas she had bought him last November, and already he was outgrowing them. She went back to the foot of the bed and took up the net again, and with the father to the left, the mother to the right, as it has always been done within the collective memory of Monisantaca, they drew the net over the whole length of their son's body, and lifted his feet to tuck it under, and they wrapped it around the rest of his body, and under the pillow in which his face was buried. They allowed him the comfort of his pillow.

"Our son sleeps soundly," said the mother. "It is perfect."

"He sleeps four dreams of tomorrow, and three of yesterday," said the father. He'd heard that said before, though he didn't know what it meant.

They pulled the net so it gathered tightly around the body of their son, but when he turned they saw they had made a serious mistake, for in the night their son and daughter had switched beds, and where they expected to see the face of Eukan Severe staring from the net, they actually saw the smiling face of Dojie Resoft, their daughter.

Sitund Monfahf rubbed his unshaven chin in confusion, and Yerml Perset folded and unfolded her hands, as if trying to wash them in the air.

"Father, Mother, what are you doing to me?" Dojie asked.

"Father? Mother?" Eukan bolted upright from a deep sleep he had finally entered after lying awake in his sister's bed for most of the night. The unfamiliar room startled him at first, but then he remembered everything, quickly dressed, slung a bag over his shoulder, and went out the door. He paused at a distance from the door to his room and saw his family in there, struggling to get Dojie out of the net. "Goodbye for now. Goodbye," he said. His eyes brimmed with tears, as he rushed down the stairs to the street. He had taken his duffel the night before, so this morning he could be swift.

As soon as his father caught a glimpse of Eukan, he turned to pursue.

"Before you go anywhere, get me out of this net," Dojie insisted.

"Why is your belly that color?" Yerml asked.

"And your back too?" Sitund pointed.

"I told you. Because this is the color that I am from now 'til forever," she said, as she leapt free. "The exact color that you are not."

Her progs turned and rushed out of the room to pursue their escaping son.

Eukan ran towards the center of town as streetlights shut off in the morning from block to block. As he trotted down the street towards the Kick, past the streetpickers scavenging cans and bottles in the morning, past streetwashers hosing down the grime, past delivery trucks tossing bundles of newspapers, he saw Ajieck in the square, talking with Ryga Yesbu, another of his gawks, and then Theki Dracanire joined him, and from behind the famous Shoe Riser, Tocst Nengl appeared. Almost all his gawks were there. He shouldn't stop, he thought. He should untie his boat and be on his way. But here was Ajieck. Was Ajieck coming with him, or not?

"Eukan, yeah, Eukan," they all said, batting their fists and the backs of their wrists together in their salute.

"What's going on, so early?" Eukan asked.

"We're waiting for Bybob Lawrek," Ajieck said.

"He's bringing the juice," said Tocst.

"What juice?" Eukan asked.

Just then Bybob came running around the corner, pushing a wheelbarrow in front of himself, containing several jugs full of something. What? It smelled like lamp oil to Eukan.

"Okay, quick, let's get this done," Ajieck said.

"Get what done?" Eukan asked.

"Someone has to do it," Ajieck said. Eukan watched them take a jug in each hand, and run over to throw it onto the Shoe Riser. They quickly soaked the whole base and splashed it against the sides, then stepped back, all but Ajieck who lifted a box of long matches in the air. "Count down," he said. Shopkeepers

STEVE KATZ

had started to unlock their gates, oblivious to what the boys were doing.

"Eight-and-a-half," Eukan's gawks all shouted. "Seven-and-a-half...six-and-a-half..." Eukan couldn't resist counting with them. "Three-and-a-half...two-and-a-half...one-and-a-half..." Ajieck struck one of the matches, then lit all the others "Ignition...one half..." Ajieck ran around the base of the Heap, tossing lit matches as he ran. "...minus one-half."

Ajieck reached Eukan, and grabbed his arm. "Come on. You've got to get going." He looked up the street. "I think I see your dad coming." Flames crept slowly through the shoe heap as they ran out of the Kick. Eukan saw his father a long way up the street. The other gawks disappeared in different directions, while Eukan and Ajieck ran to the wharf. Ajieck stopped by the pile of his stuff he had removed from the boat.

"Get in. I'll push you off."

"What is this?" Eukan asked.

"It's my stuff. You said you don't want me to come, so I'm..."

Eukan started to toss Ajieck's gear back into the boat. He'd had other things on his mind, so he hadn't thought about this, but he knew deep down he didn't want to go anywhere without Ajieck.

"You're stealing my stuff," Ajieck said.

"Shut up, and get your stuff in the boat," Eukan shoved him.

Black smoke rose behind them.

"Eukan, Eukan Severe," his father shouted, running down the wharf.

He and Ajieck tossed the rest of everything into the boat, and Eukan untied the bow, and they both jumped in as Sitund

132

got closer. Behind his head, flames from the Kick started to lick the rising sun.

"Eukan Severe! What do you think you're doing?" Sitund dove and grabbed the rope at the stern. "Who gave you permission to do this?"

"We are your parents," Yerml complained, as she arrived just behind her husband.

Eukan pulled a leather sheath from his duffel, and raised it above his head. It was the *clenac jectorp*, given him by his grandfather just before he died. "I unsheathe thee now," Eukan declared, his voice cracking with adolescence for the last time. He pulled the saber from the sheath, jumped to the point of the stern and with one swing cut through the thick rope. His father's hand was nicked by the blade, and he brought the blood to his lips.

"Ahhh, my son," cried the father.

All the sirens of Monisantaca were wailing, and Ajieck pulled out his trombone to join them with one long sliding note. Dojie arrived at the wharf, followed by many of her brideys, and all of their gawks lined up at the riverside now to wish Eukan and Ajieck safe travel.

"We love you, Eukan Severe, brother mine," Dojie shouted as she followed the boat. She tossed a neatly wrapped bundle that bounced off the side, and into the water. "Get them," she shouted. "My gift, just for you." Ajieck laid his belly across the gunwale and with an oar flipped the packet into the air so Eukan could grab it, then he tore open the packet. His heart convulsed as he showed the contents to Ajieck. It was *warmworms*, *phroa warmworms*. This was the first time his sister had ever given him any. He jumped up and down, and waved, and blew kisses at her. Dojie and all her brideys followed them as far as they could, skating laterally along the riverwalk, blowing kisses across the water.

As they drifted down the river the young men leaned against the starboard side of the little boat, and watched Monisantaca retreat from them. Black smoke rose from the smoldering Shoe Riser and, as if in sympathy, Bysbu volcano behind the town sent up puffs of its own, white steam clean as a dream.

"Why did you do that? Why did you burn it?" Eukan asked Ajieck, as they both looked back, their eyes wet with tears.

"I told you, someone had to do it," said Ajieck. "Now it will burn forever."

"Forever is a long time," said Eukan Severe.

"Not if you live only once," Ajieck Nach responded, then he slapped the wall of the boat. "What do we call this *boat*? I want to call it *Rylinma Noorem*, so beautiful and delicious and so sexy. And you built it. And we're on it."

"It's called *Etatreh*," Eukan said.

"You're so serious, so serious about everything. We should give it a sexy woman's name. *Mau Ruthnam*, for instance. Something to keep us going."

"Well. I was almost cooked into a barbecue, boy," Eukan grinned. "I think that's serious. This boat comes from an ancient source; it's like…it's sacred."

Ajieck shook his head, stroked his chin. "Well…okay, Eukan. Serious it is. This is great. *Etatreh* it is!" With unparalleled agility he jumped up and balanced on the gunwales as he danced around the boat several times. "This feels so great," he cried, and then he turned to the town that was almost out of sight. "Listen, you sons of bitches," he boomed, raising his trombone above his head.

And thus began the independent blockbuster lives of Eu-kan Severe and Ajieck Nach, chilling and audacious, brazen, dynamic, sometimes relentlessly funny lives of sheer dynamite and devilishly good fun, lives that made them legends in their own time. And thus we know them today from their many fea-tures and all their sequels.

be continued...

THE DERIVATION OF THE KISS

It was nineteen sixty-nine, in Iowa City,
And I was there. This was not a pretty
Place, but it had some qualities
I enjoyed; a bookstore called Quiddity's
For one, where I went to browse at night,
One tall red-headed clerk, on whom my sight
Was set. It took a while, but that was fine.
I was sure that eventually I'd get to dine
With her at someplace excellent and snug
Where we could intimately converse. It bugs
Me now that I can't remember her name.
Let's call her Helen. I make no real claim
On her memory except that she was there
When this stuff happened that I want to share
With all of you, who I'm sure have paid the price
Of glimpsing Hell when you aim for paradise.

That night I dressed up some, my beloved Borsalino
Crushable hat, bought in Verona, and pressed chino
Pants I wore when I wanted my image to dip
South of hippy. The eatery recommended was a trip
Over dark Iowa roads to another tiny town
And there we ate small birds, like quail browned
And sauced sweet with oranges, and then we talked
Nothings over chocolate cake, and at last we walked
Back out into the Iowa small-town autumn night

STEVE KATZ

Into the smell of harvest and the distant light
Of pig sheds. I breathed in an America I never knew;
Helen stretched a stiff arm to my shoulder, breathed in too,
And suggested we return to Iowa City, where a band...
She knew the drummer, and the singer, and they'd planned
To meet where they played, at the club called Mother's.
We'd get in free, she said. The band was like brothers
To her, she'd known them for so long. We could drink
And dance, and get the evening over with is what I think
She thinks. Am I so boring in my chinos and Borsalino hat,
I wonder; but the evening's trials reached way beyond that.

It was still as a swamp in Iowa City when we returned,
A dank haze off the river. A few street lamps burned,
Dimmer than darkness; the small houses shrunk back
Into their lawns. Outside the club, a long row of black
Choppers leaned on kickstands, watched by one dull
Rider—D.T. Eagles, Chicago, Illinois, around a skull-
And-crossbones, on his leather jacket. His vacant eye
Sucked down on us as a leech onto a wader's thigh.
"This shit looks very deep," I whispered to my dinner date.
"So? I'm going in anyway," she told me. "I'm already late."
Late for what, I thought; nonetheless, I bundled all my fears
And followed Helen in, as I've done for thousands of years.

Admission was free, as Helen had promised. The air
Was gray and stupid with demons. The band took a fair
Stab at happy rock-and-roll. I stood spooked at the door
A moment, then slid inside. On the darkened dance floor
Two bikers, pants at ankles, dipped each other's fudge.
I held onto my hat, as the saying goes, and didn't budge

From my spot against a post. This was no way romantic.
I saw Helen nowhere. Against the wall some frantic
Undergraduate couples, all dressed up, were trapped
In a booth as bikers climbed the boothbacks and snapped
Belts at them and pissed into their beer. When the band
Wanted a break, all the bikers turned, each raising a hand
In fascist salute. *Sieg Heil! Sieg Heil! Sieg Heil!* Until
They played again. It was a triumph of the bikers' will.
I remembered noticing, as we drove into town, the police
Station, usually well-lit, was asleep, cops hiding in the crease
Of their disadvantage. I saw Helen now crouched behind
The drummer. She didn't look for me. Never mind.
Her pal was six-foot-six, and black, and very wide,
Certainly more fit and eligible than I to save her hide.

Then it happened as in confusion I was standing there
That one good gentleman of the D.T. Eagles came to stare
Into my face. He was a smaller, sober officer of their dim
Celebration, who held a garbage bag of pills. From him
His cohorts grabbed a random mix of 'ludes, white crosses,
Black beauties, pinks and blues, and by handfuls tossed
Them down like mindwarp jelly beans. His eyes laced
Red with grim mischief, he removed my Borsalino, placed
His greasy leather snapbrim on my brow and donned
My dear fedora. Goodbye, Borsalino. I was stupidly fond
Of that hat, but didn't know what to do to get it back.
The dark gentleman, I never learned his name, Jack
We'll call him, strutted around the room under his new
Loot. I was powerless beneath his leather cap, when two
Snorting bikers several semis wide arrived in my face.
"That hat, where the fuck did you…" This growl could erase

Six books of *Paradise Lost*. "It's all right," someone said,
Lucky for me. "He's Jack's boy," making me sound dead.

But to my relief, indeed my glee, it turned out Jack
Was an honest biker. He circulated twice then gave it back
To me. My Borsalino on my head again, on his the leather cap.
He was happy, and I felt some blithe uneasiness. Then a tap
On my shoulder made me turn to see another wretched soul
Trapped as myself, a young man who tried to take the role
Of adviser. He whispered, "You'd better hide that hat under
Your jacket." He seemed competent. How bad a blunder
This could be I didn't realize. Anyone outside my meek
Self was welcome to construct my fate. Hide the hat and sneak
Away. This was at least a plan. Inside this club the weather
Warped with anarchy, an oily stink of sweat and leather.
The D.T. Eagles danced together. Helen hidden; myself, alone.
Jack was here, his smile sinister and sweet. He pierced the bone
Of my face with his stare. "Why don't you make me a gift
Of that hat?" He'd seen me. He grabbed my beard to lift
My gaze to his eyes. Nothing I could do then. The hat
Was his. I understood the code I'd broken. That was that.
Hiding would be chickenshit in my own neighborhood.
I opened up my jacket, he took the hat for good.

Was I man enough, I wondered, to get beaten to the bone
For my Borsalino? I could see my obits written in stone,
WRITER DIES PROTECTING CRUSHABLE FEDORA,
ITALIAN HATS BACK IN FASHION!, my soul an aurora
Of dread. I could die, risking humiliation and death
Before I finished my second novel. No! Jack's breath
Suddenly engulfed my face again. No! His beard brushed

Through mine, tongue struck into my mouth, lips crushed
My lips, the reek of beer and leather and my own fear
Of this hideous humiliation, at the same time an unclear
Thought that maybe now he'd give me… I'd get my hat
Back, and I could leave, to feed my just invented cat.
So feeble, my only strength was in that miserable kiss,
And then a recognition—this was not bad, not the bliss
I was looking for, but you can't always get what you want.
He put his head on my shoulder, and whispered, "I want
You to ride with me." The band was quiet. It was late.
Reverberations of his whisper thundered down my fate.
This was an opportunity I could easily resist though not
Easily avoid. Jack left me thinking. I inched off my spot.

Now it seems impossible I got out of there by moving
Slowly to the door; that Jack let me go, never proving
How much he wanted me to ride with him. Perhaps a guy
Without a Borsalino is less conspicuous. Out the door, I fly
To my car, grin once at the guard snoozing by their bikes,
Dive to the seat, key, fire, YES, my car, a Lancia I really like.
The advance from *Posh*, my Grove Press book of porn,
Bought this sleekness, cherrywood-steering, operatic horn.

What I have told here is the origin of the kiss, on page
Five hundred and thirty-two of *Swanny's Ways*,
My novel, winner 1995 America Award in fiction
Which you can check out, if reading is your predilection.
If you're curious did I ever kiss Helen, I can't remember.
I could have once, maybe later, maybe in December.

DATE BITING

The practice of date-biting becomes a problem with the new generation of SEDs (Sexual Enhancement Drugs). These advanced versions—Pyogra, Bialis, and Lolitro—affect both male potency and female receptivity. With their advent, the prevalence of date-biting has increased substantially and is expected to spread and grow in intensity as generic equivalents hit the market. The improved stimulators perk up sexual desire, extend the period of lubrication in the female, and allow the male to produce an erection lasting four hours and thirty-four minutes (the present record) without danger of degenerative priapism. An additional benefit of this new generation of SEDs is a marked improvement in passionate vocalizing. A twosome of elderly subjects no longer need sound like two geezers croaking in the desiccated pond scum, but can chime sweetly musical tunes as if they were principals in an operetta by Victor Herbert.

An alarm sounded, however, when doctors from all over the United States, and particularly from both coasts, reported increasing numbers of senior trauma victims with analogous masticatory woundings. We soon began to suspect this was a collateral effect of the new SEDs. Early testers had observed that the gerbils on which the drug was first tested took to gnawing on each other, occasionally snipping a jugular. The testers dismissed this as insignificant, or as a practice peculiar to gerbil culture.

There had been some severe infections in the human population, and a few minor amputations—here a nose, there an ear or a lip, even half a penis in San Francisco, but no more than might be expected from commonplace, if extreme, amatory enthusiasms. No serious deaths were recorded until Mr. Benjamin Hackle found the jugular of his romantic other, the elderly Sylvia Marsh. He claims that it wasn't intentional, and that for her this had been an amative ending to a long, happy life. The question arose then of who was responsible, Hackle or the drug company. Of course the drug company denies any liability, and Hackle claims the song was great, wiping a tear of regret—at the last a flatted fifth, just like in the jazz she loved (he plays baritone).

Youths, both prepubescent and full-blown teenagers, have already taken to the drug, and it is too late to prohibit it because they have learned to fabricate an equivalent out of used phone cards, steamed, dried, and pulverized, combined with wasabi, the juice of fermented seafood, and the hair of the Shih Tzu. In 500mg capsules sold on the street, this works as well for them as the drug company formulate, at least, as far as its effect on the young voice in the throes of passion. For the passion itself they don't need extra stimulation. It is the youth who gave date-biting its name. They appropriated it from a song written for the hip-hop band, *Purlee Wightz*, by its two lead singers, Y'diz and JnJo, brothers who grew up in the ghetto of Toledo. Their father was the first dentist on Dorr Street. The song topped the hip-hop charts for several weeks. Wounding has hardly been observed in the young because they have been educated to understand the perils of blood and other bodily fluids. The activity manifests as a furiously playful nibbling, light in its effect. Unlike the hickeys of yesteryear, it doesn't leave the shape of the perpetrator's teeth on the neck or wherever, but can create a broad region of bruised skin. Even this is quite beautiful on the young body; in fact, they often display their amorous road maps through holes they cut in their clothes, and they recognize each other as nibblers by the clicking of teeth that punctuates their rhyming bouts as they stimulate each other at their raves. Sometimes thousands of nibblers gather under one roof. So many have taken vows of celibacy 'til marriage that the condoms that responsible sponsors distribute generally go unused. Abstinence has, in fact, become so cool, that even in the affluent white teenybopper population, where kids hardly need to abstain from anything, nothing-doing is the rule. The subtler pleasure of doing nothing, they say, is way more cool. However, many of the kids have started to sharpen their teeth, and we have to watch that phenomenon.

The problems are exacerbated among people in young adulthood or early middle age. Though people at the height of their earning powers and sexual prowess might have immense holdings, their needs are almost always greater. At certain hours of the early morning whole complexes of singles—condos, co-ops, duplexes, studios—seem to lift off their lots in a chorus of top ten favorites, or a mellow treatment in the new torch song, crooner revival, or even something surprisingly operatic like the counter-tenor, mezzo soprano duet from act two of Philip Glass' *Akhnaten*, or the seduction duet from Mozart's *Don Giovanni*—*La ci darem la mano...vorrei e non vorrei*. For me it is an auditory ravishment to stroll among the dwellings of the swinging singles, or the young marrieds, or even the suburban houses of established families renewing their passions. As for myself, I have left sexual activity behind to pursue the contemplative life and to work for the general good. My fillip is to wander through a community of busy lovers. It's the gorgeous part of my life. I stroll as if through a forest of rare songbirds. I pleasure myself at this in the evening. My colleague tells me that certain week-end afternoons are even more delightful.

Not so long ago I began to notice another sound, like an unamused *hah*, coming from certain of the dwellings. At first it was just an occasional burst, but then it became so frequent that it sounded like the rattling of an automatic weapon, or the *Kec!cac* of the Balinese monkey chant. From my informants I discovered that this curious noise, this static, was due to an alarming practice that had manifested among the people in this age group. It spread there like grease on a griddle. What the kids called date-biting, and themselves express as harmless nibbling has evolved in these adults into a practice of biting off small hunks of their partners and swallowing them in a spasm of gullet rapture. The interference of the swallowing with the sound of the voice produces the *hah hah hah hah* I keep hearing. The practice, I hear, has spread into the nightlife where the younger adults mark themselves, or have close friends mark them where they can't reach, to indicate what they are willing to offer to a potential mate. As I understand it, the practice is not to chew, but to swallow as if you are taking an oyster down the throat.

Perhaps this is the explanation for what I have noticed of late in pharmacies, that there has appeared a great variety of do-it-yourself wound-stitching kits. After making love these people don't spend their time as we once did, lying back and relaxing in the wet spot, or smoochily conversing, or lighting a cigarette, but they now busy themselves cleaning the datebites, and suturing. The attractions of this whole gestalt might explain why the teenagers are sharpening their teeth—in anticipation of their maturity.

For whatever it is worth, this practice has limited itself thus far to North America, and there, mostly to the United States. It does show up a bit in Canada, where people have become less likely lately to follow American fashion. In Mexico, at popular vacation venues like Mazatlán, Cancun, Acapulco, Puerto Vallarta, the resorts are happy to accommodate the practice, but it is not attractive to the Mexicans themselves. At Playa Carmen it is forbidden. In general, the Europeans don't do it. They are content with the time-tested more traditional modes of exacerbating their pleasures. In some places in the Orient this practice is punishable by death.

I use the "D" word cautiously, because this outcome is not likely, though not impossible. A heads up is in order, because the human mouth is rife with toxins. The bite of a human can be deadly, either from a transmitted disease, or, as we have already seen, the careless snipping of a jugular. So far there have been recorded few serious injuries, and far fewer fatalities. For the sake of freedom, adults should not be prohibited from following their passions in the privacy of their own boudoirs. In service to the general good, myself and my friend Mathilde Al-Sarhan ben Gorsky are keeping our eyes and ears peeled, and will inform of any serious developments.

WING NIGHT

THE WHITE PAGES

It was Wing Night at the Hoff. In the first two weeks of
August the pub is always packed. Many people visit from away.
Some come home for family gatherings, some are back in Inverness for the first time after many years, back at the shores
where their grandparents once homesteaded. Some casual
tourists, as well, add their bulk and appetites to a crowd of local regulars who suck on chicken wings every Thursday, regular or spicy or honey-garlic. This is the notorious Inverness
Saloon, fixed above the former coal mines as asylum for the
lonely and the parched on the western shore, the sunset shore
of Cape Breton Island. Many come to observe friends perform,
or to perform themselves in the karaoke MC'd by Elaina Brody.
Several regulars malinger in the Paddock, to shoot pool, or sit
themselves down in front of the poker machines to lose their
money. Earlier in the week two American women who have
summer homes at the Broad Cove Banks advertised in the local
weekly that they would be performing their special karaoke this
very Thursday night, and they challenged all comers, as if they
understood karaoke as a game, a zero-sum competition. One
is Wren Queasy from California, the other Molly Plumpt from
Pennsylvania. They hover near the stage and comment to each
other that the crowd is even greater than they had anticipated,
and agree that this is a terrific response to the notice of their
appearance.

Candy and Colin sit close to the bar, on the far side of the partition away from the stage. Candy sips a Captain Morgan and Coke, slowly getting soused to catch up with her boyfriend. She runs her right pinky down the pages of Elaina's song list. "I can do 'Sixteen Tons,'" she declares.

"A man sings that one," says Colin, leaning like a sapling against the wind of a three-day drunk.

Emily Klusziewski delivers their chicken wings and another round of drinks. She is the daughter of Harry Klusziewski, son of Polish immigrants. Her grandfather had a small farm near the ocean on Broad Cove Marsh. Now someone else owns the farm, and raises bison, and occasionally slaughters one to sell the good meat at MacLellan's Grocery. She is back to work for the summer even though her family has moved to Manitoba. She hopes to save enough money to go back for her sophomore year at St. Mary's in Halifax.

"What do you think?" Candy asks her. "'Sixteen Tons' or what?"

"Why not?" Emily smiles then rushes away.

"You gotta have the do-jigger down there to sing 'Sixteen Tons,'" Colin shouts after her.

"I beg your pardon." Candy fends him from slumping against her with the forearm of her hand that holds the pages. "I'm not gonna grow any little winker just so I can sing my song."

"Tons," Colin mumbles.

On the verandah looking out to sea across the old slag heaps of the coal mine—that have recently been covered with topsoil, and planted with grass—Alice sits with a vodka and cranberry, and her husband Kevin, with a beer, a Keith's. "I can't get used to looking at this grass. It's not normal. I don't think it looks any better."

"I never look at it."

"Whoever thought I would miss the old dump? At least you could remember there were jobs here once. And how pitiful is golf? What's golf got to do with our Inverness? Too windy here, anyway. Not enough calm days to make a golf course."

"I'll buy some clubs."

"With what?"

"A little putter. A little driver. I would go out and fish for a living if there were some fish left. The fish is gone, probably forever. No more cod, by God. And my grandfather Beaton was a farmer. I'll get me a little nine iron." From his seat he does a cramped golf swing, then he tips the bottle over his lips, and beer spills down the sides of his mouth.

"I need something." Alice slides slowly off the edge of the bench. She's a big, soft woman, several folds of flesh over the belt of her grey jeans. She rises with a sigh and heads towards the door, stops and turns back to her man. "Spicy, or regular?"

"Keith's," Kevin says.

A gaggle of young men, a few years past drinking age, home from college in Antigonish, or Halifax, or Quebec, or Ontario, reminisce with slaps on the back, and hugs, and stories of great drinking bouts at school, fights that broke out, girls that were out of control. "He hit me so hard I folded over, but then I straightened up and caught his jaw with my skull, and he flew over the table." He slaps his temple. "My head is good for something." The young women talk animatedly among themselves, but keep an eye on the guys. They talk wedding preparations, printed invitations, supper in the fire hall, wedding gowns. Some say they can't think about marriage yet, not until they finish school, settle on a career and a job. Katie, whose father has an alcohol problem and is abusive, will never marry, not to some guy. She looks over at the men with an expression of disgust. Later she will sing at the karaoke. Each will sing a specialty, the song for which she is famous in their group.

Gordon the bartender watches some young men come in from the parking lot. He recognizes that these puppies are from Port Hood, and that could mean trouble. Young beef from Port Hood sometimes look for a battle when they get a little too lubricated in Inverness. After all, Al MacGinnis is from Port Hood, and he is a hockey hero. What do the Invernessers have to recommend themselves at all? Gordon makes a mental note to keep an eye on this.

Alice squeezes her way through the crowd towards the bar. She glimpses the two American women who hang lewdly from the pillars as if they are working their libidos at a titty bar. They look middle-aged, she thinks. And the more they try not to look so, the more they do. They leap to the stage and with Molly holding and humping Wren from behind they start to sing Madonna's "Material Girl." *Way bad*, Alice thinks. Madonna was bad enough. "She's my bitch. She's my bitch. She's my bitch," Molly humps and chants below the song. She wears a red jersey, and a red baseball cap at an angle that might be called hip-hop. Wren wears a kilt, and that makes Alice uneasy. "Fuck 'em." The women charge the comfortable brown gloom of the club with a wicked energy that offends Alice in a way she can't define. Maybe it's the kilt. She stops Emily and orders the spicy wings, a vodka and cranberry, and a Keith's. She doesn't act very friendly to Emily, even though Emily used to babysit for her. Maybe, Emily thinks, it is because her father used to work with Alice's dad, on the highway maintenance crew, and Emily's father was found stealing diesel fuel from the county, for his own dozer and excavator, for his own stillborn construction company. That was one reason her family moved to Manitoba. She had come back this summer to be with her high school friends, but she might as well have worked in Halifax. It wasn't as friendly for her here as she had hoped.

Wren is pumped, and ready to sing all night. She's never worn her kilt in Cape Breton before. She bought it several years back at a yard sale near Albany. It is a clan MacDougall tartan, though she never knew that till recently. Her buddy, Molly, thinks she looks cute in the kilt, and enjoys humping her from behind as any man might. This is Molly's first summer in her new house on Broad Cove Banks and she is having a ball relaxing and partying in this beautiful spot. She shouts "Bitch bitch bitch. She's my bitch." She enjoys mouthing the word, and explains into the mic that she is using that word because…because… She doesn't have the words to explain why, but she does think she is greasing the evening in this Cape Breton maritime town with some U.S. ghetto hip-hop attitude.

In its turn-of-the-century glory, Inverness was a tough coal-mining town. People from all over the world worked here. The town has seen all forms of human weirdness and courage and kindness, and tolerates almost anything.

On the verandah the young men are mingling with the young women now, speaking to each other in hushed tones, as they watch the sunset together. Layers of violet and green slowly darken over the water.

"Tonight I think it's the Perseid," Andrew says.

"What's that, Perseid?" asks the slightly tipsy Lillian, who leans into Andrew, her hand on his shoulder.

"It's a meteor shower. Every year this time."

"Good," says Malcolm, sometimes called Mud because he's always at the bottom of the scrum when he plays rugby for St. Mary's. "Andy needs a shower, to clean up." Mud has been trying to chat up Lillian all evening because he'd heard she was hot, but her attraction to Andrew becomes more pronounced as she drinks more.

"I don't think we'll be able to see much from here, though. Too much artificial light."

"You can see me. I'm altogether here. All of me is here." She presses closer, lips puckering.

"Shower. Meteor. Get it?" Mud mumbles, disheartened. He looks into the scrum of women for another candidate, and slides away.

Emily slips past Malcolm, her arms full of wing baskets. He grabs at her ass and misses. He remembers who she is, Harry K…whatever's daughter, the daughter of a thief. That makes her kind of sexy. And she looks better than she did in high school. A little plump, and hot. Dark. Sultry.

"She's wearin' a fuckin' kilt," Alice says, setting the wings down. She slides the beer into Kevin's hand.

"It's a plaid skirt, that's all it is." Kevin sucks a wing to the bone, then sticks the bone up a nostril and looks around for laughs.

"With the goddam *sporran* it's a goddam kilt. It's the Mac-Dougall tartan, yours, and that pouch is probably worth more than your pickup."

Kevin twists a bone into his other nostril and stands up. "MacInnis tartan. Show me where she is. I'll slap her with my pouch."

"MacDougall, you nitwit. I don't like it one bit. Not even Scottish, I don't think."

Kevin sneezes the bones back into the wing basket. "Keith's," he says, lifting the bottle.

Emily scours the verandah for empties, which she throws into an Oland's carton.

"Isn't that Emily what's-her-name?" Stacey MacMaster whispers to Nancy Ross. "Her father...you know."

"I think you're right," Nancy whispers.

"I never could pronounce her name. Look at her."

Emily tries to get past Mud, who won't let her pass. He stares at her. "I knew your father," he says, which isn't true. She fakes right, and goes left around him. He stumbles and falls against a table. It bums her to be reminded of her father.

Alexander Goldfarb and his wife, Hilda, step cautiously through the pub door. Neither of them spends much time in bars at home in New York state. He is in his mid-fifties, has taken an early retirement from a state college where he taught in departments of Communication and Education. He sports a trimmed, graying beard, and a bushy moustache carefully shaped to cover a slight harelip.

"It looks like Jewish food in here," Hilda whispers to her husband. A big 'fro of curly brown hair surrounds her be-mused, mousy face, twitching above a stooped body that seems to shrink as you watch.

"What do you mean?"

"It's brown in here, like stuffed derma, or pot roast and kasha. Jewish food is always brown."

"Hmmm." Her husband nods, narrowing his eyes to look around. The couple is on a quest. They have been coming to Cape Breton every summer for several years, looking for a special piece of land to enjoy in their retirement, preferably near the shore, preferably with a beach, and not too expensive. They know the bargain days are over. They have to live within the limitations of their resources, but they are willing to pay something. The deep cocoa atmosphere of the pub feels odd, and the activity, the karaoke, intimidates them. Hilda disappears to look for the bathroom, leaving Alexander to fend for himself. A young woman in a mini squeezes in next to him at the bar and places her heavily ringed hand on his cheek.

"Ya look like Colonel Sanders." She waves at the bartender. "I need another drink, but Gordon, he doesn't like me." Her wild blonde hair unnerves Alexander, and the pressure of her thigh against his crotch. "Ya do look like Colonel Sanders, ya know."

"Thank you," Alexander says, and then boldly, "I am Colonel Sanders."

On the stage a paunchy man about Alexander's age dressed in an ill-fitting tweed jacket, with a clip-on bowtie dangling from his open collar, struggles through Johnny Cash's "I Walk the Line." He looks to be in pain.

"Thank you, kind sir, that's right. I knew it, soon as I seen ya. I'm not drunk. Thank you," repeats the young blonde. "So now ya have to divorce yer wife and marry me, and then ya have to die and leave me all yer money."

Alexander looks around to see if Hilda is back yet. "So what do I get out of it?" He is proud to have the courage to say anything at all.

"This one's yer wife?" Hilda has returned. "He's going to marry me." She lets go of his arm. "After he divorces you." She grabs the rum and 7UP Gordon set down by her hand. "Yiz from away, the two of yiz. That's perfectly goosy. That's goosy gander." As she turns to leave she says, "But I'm gonna have the Colonel's money." Alexander watches her stagger out to the verandah, flattening the back of her denim mini with her free hand.

"How about some wings?" Alexander asks his wife.

"Chicken wings?" Hilda watches her new rival on the verandah flirting with some young men in baseball caps. Not really a rival, she thinks; but it makes her feel too old to be at the Hoff.

Cameron Fitzgerald comes in the door with his fiddle case under his arm, as he does frequently on Thursday nights. He's pushing ninety but there is an echo of former jauntiness in his step. He often mistakes karaoke night for an old-fashioned ceilidh, an opportunity to screech his fiddle. He can play with some verve for an old guy, but has never made a sound anyone would voluntarily listen to. One could say he has lost it, but perhaps he never had it. Gordon signals to two of the regulars. They approach him, one taking his fiddle case, the other gently cradling his elbow. "Come, Cameron. Sit with us."

Molly leans over Candy and Colin, and turns her red cap from an angle to the right, to an angle to the left. "Come on. Do something. Join in. It's fun. Sing a song." On the stage Wren takes the mic to sing "Mustang Sally," Wilson Pickett, her favorite.

"I'll sing as fuckin' soon as I'm fuckin' ready to sing. You go sing for yer fuckin' self."

"She'll sing 'Sixteen Tons.'"

"I'll sing twenty-seven tons. I'll sing as many fuckin' tons as I want to."

Molly skips back to the stage, to join her partner. Wren taps on the mic. It's off. It is almost eleven, last call for wings. Elaina Brody, a pert pretty blonde, in a crepe mini, emerges from behind her booth and takes the microphone. Her karaoke begins officially after she sings her first song. The rest was all warm-up. She poses a moment with the mike, hips thrust provocatively to one side, and starts her evening with "Strawberry Wine," a song about losing your innocence at seventeen. She has a throaty, mature voice, and carries the song like a backpack into the ghetto. The young men tipping bottles of Keith's and Blue down their throats look at her with some yearning, and all of them know it will take more than some sips of strawberry wine by the riverside to convince her to yield her innocence again.

Karaoke brings out the party in people, not just in Wren and Molly, who rise again to the stage to sing. Elaina has to tell them politely that she has a list, and the first on that list is one of the favorite local divas, Tessa Besoin, who usually sings "Beautiful," the Christina Aguilera song, and Tessa is one of the most beautiful of the young women. Gordon puts down his towel, stops drying glasses to watch her. "Tessa! Tessa! Tessa!" people shout from all over the room. Her mother, who hardly ever goes to the Hoff, stands up to applaud with a chicken bone dangling like a cigarette from her lips. In her low-cut red dress, she reveals a lovely bosom of which she is proud. She looks down to make sure her cleavage is nicely visible, then applauds her daughter.

Kids crowd the verandah door to hear Tessa. Seeing her, though he hardly knows her, makes Jamie weep. He does know she is a great stepdancer, has seen her do it, and now she is studying ballet. He recently graduated in computer engineering, and has no idea if he will find a job or not. He doesn't get it, why he has these emotions. He would gladly have stayed and fished with his dad, but his dad recently sold off his lobster-fishing tags. Jamie always thought fishing lobster was something he could fall back on, instead of sitting in a cubicle and staring at a computer screen. The lobster will go the way of the cod, and the crab will soon go too. "What the fuck," he wipes his eyes and listens to Tessa. "I'll get drunk." He finishes his beer, and picks up the rum and Coke that has been left on the table near him. Maybe it belongs to someone who is dancing. The dance floor has started to fill up. He throws it down anyway.

While Tessa sings, Gordon comes out from back of the bar and skillfully nudges an incipient fight, between a Port Hood boyo and an Inverness boyo, out the door to the parking lot. Billy Crump smiles as he watches Gordon operate. He is almost always smiling. You have to smile if you spend your life with chickens. His wife will get here after the babysitter is settled. She likes to belt out a Dixie Chicks song, like "Wide Open Spaces," or "Landslide," though she often looks for something Canadian too, like Alanis Morissette, like Avril Lavigne, like Hank Snow, like Gordon Lightfoot or k.d. lang. She likes them a lot, but not to sing their songs herself. Anne Murray, even, who came from Cape Breton is always a possibility. She usually ends up singing Dixie Chicks, however. Maybe it's because they raise chickens, Billy chuckles. These are free-range chickens, broiler pullets that put on four pounds in seven weeks, three months 'til market. He distributes to all the co-ops, to restaurants all over the island. Hundreds of chickens. When Billy closes his eyes all he sees is chickens, feathered and plump. Leonard Cohen! If Billy sang he would sing a Leonard Cohen song. "Bird on the Wire." Billy doesn't sing, however.

Marilyn Goo-goo comes in the door alone, slipping by the altercation in the parking lot. She always comes alone from the rez, because she doesn't want to ask anyone to come with her. Since she moved back to the reservation after law school she occasionally has the urge to do what the white people do. She doesn't even enjoy this, but she has spent so much time with white people in school, in her sorority, in her first law firm, where she easily passed as Portuguese or Iranian, that she still occasionally needs a white fix. At school and with her law firm she went by the name of Marilyn Gehry, because she didn't want to have to explain Goo-goo, not that she was ashamed of it. She always thought that if she hadn't seen more of a need for lawyers among her people, she might have been an architect. She has never done a song, though she has a great voice. She thinks she can do something by Rita Coolidge. Billy Crump smiles at her as she orders a Moosehead from Gordon. She ignores him, not wanting to engage anyone in conversation. No one, she thinks, will ever call her a red apple.

"So this poor guy hanged himself from the bridge, middle of last winter. Middle of a snow storm." Marvin Allen tells Emery this story he just heard from Tessa Besoin's mother, Crispi. He can't tell if Emery is listening. Emery is Wren's husband. He is concentrating on Wren as she runs around like a simpleton;

in fact, he is shooting a video of her shenanigans. Maybe he will show it to her later, Marvin thinks, once she is sober. Emery is a recovering alcoholic, so he doesn't drink. He is also an artist, as is his wife, so perhaps this video will be part of a performance. "He didn't know anything about hanging someone, so he used chicken wire around his neck. My friend said her dogs were going crazy for two days, and she didn't know why. The poor bozo was hanging there for two days before they found him." Marvin thinks that perhaps Emery has nothing to say.

Wren and Molly are back at the mic, ready to sing Fats Domino's "Blueberry Hill," when suddenly most of their audience rises and rushes to the window like flies to a smear of honey. The tension and macho display that has been slowly building, between the Port Hood and Inverness men, has finally erupted into a fistfight that goes full-blast now in the parking lot, two big males rolling across the blacktop, smashing each other. Their friends whistle, egg them on.

"They're hurting each other," says Leon Kimmel, a transplant to Cape Breton from Windsor, Ontario. He is an ecologist, a green guy, proactive in the fight against pesticides and seismic testing, who runs a sugarbush on his land, and takes serious photographs.

"Fuck do you expect?" says the guy next to him. "It's a goddamned fight."

Leon feels himself nudged towards the door by the crowd trying to get out. He came to the Hoff just because he was curious about Wing Night, and karaoke. Fists flying is not his idea of a fun evening.

"...on blueberry hill," Molly and Wren sing anyway. "...on blueberry hill...when I found you." They watch the crowd melt away from the window, as the combatants shove back in through the door, slightly bloodied, clothes ripped up, their arms around each other's shoulders. They belly up to the bar for their next beer.

If they are going to fight, Emily thinks, they should do it for something that matters. She delivers three baskets of wings and a pitcher of beer to a table of heavyset women who have come to eat and drink. None of these women will sing, though a couple of them sometimes dance.

Emily had been in Quebec for the WTO protest, and she had been briefly arrested, but her friend Brendan had been smacked with a nightstick. He still gets headaches. She tries to tell people about that, but no one here is interested, at least, not among her high school friends. They are interested in getting drunk and getting laid. She is glad to be back here if only to learn that about everybody. It will be a kind of closure.

Leon slips out the door, and drives his Volvo back into the night.

Marilyn Goo-goo pages through the song list—so many songs, and nothing yet by Rita Coolidge.

As Jamie heads from the window back to the verandah, Candy grabs him by the leg of his shorts. "Jamie, you know all about this. You go to school. I want to sing 'Sixteen Tons,' but Colin don't want me to."

"That's a man's song anyway, for a man to sing," Colin says without looking up.

Jamie lays a hand on Colin's head. "Well, she's a kind of a man, Colin. She's a candyman. She buys the drinks, don't she?"

"That's right, sing 'Candy Man,'" Colin says, looking in her face. Jamie removes Candy's hand from his pants, and heads back to the verandah. "You going to play a few tunes?" he asks as he passes old Cameron Fitzgerald, who sits with his fiddle case open, plucking the strings. "Yass," says Cameron, "They're fixin' the sound. As soon as they fix it."

"So the guy, I think this happened because he had come here loving some woman in town—he didn't know anything about hanging himself—and that's how he decided to use chicken wire. No one in town knew him real well. I don't think he came from down here. He was quite a heavy man anyway, and when they found him..." Marvin suddenly remembers that Emery is a Vietnam vet, and possibly suffers from post-traumatic stress, and has seen worse than this, and probably blocks it out. He suddenly feels bad, but is compelled to finish the story. There is some pleasure he takes in telling it: "So all that was dangling off the bridge there was the head and the spine. The rest was gone. When Sandy, the poor Mountie on duty, went to investigate he didn't know what he was looking at. They thought maybe some coyotes had jumped up and grabbed the rest of the body for their dinner, but then they found the whole mess further down the brook. All the flesh had sort of slumped off like an overcoat."

Emery has no response, as if he isn't listening. Molly and Wren prance by on the dance floor. They are trying to lead a parade, a samba line, a bunny-hop. They pull people up to the dance floor. Emery will not dance. Marvin will, though he has no partner. Molly works out on a pillar as if she is advertising lap dances. Alexander and Hilda shuffle onto the far corner of the dance floor. Stacey MacMaster is called in from the verandah for her turn to sing Shania Twain's "Don't Be Stupid (You Know I Love You)." "This is more like it," Hilda says. She closes her eyes to get into the beat, bites her lower lip, shakes her curly hair to the music. Rodney Frasier lunges onto the dance floor, followed by Mary, his wife, who grabs him by his belt, his shirtsleeve, whatever she can, to keep him from falling into people. The stroke he suffered a few months back has made his movement spastic, out of control, and reduced his voice to some grunts and moans that only Mary understands. His infirmity arrived with a new love for dancing, square or social. Before the stroke he had never shown an interest, but now he dances at every opportunity, thrashing about the floor to some people's amusement, and others' chagrin.

Alexander Goldfarb doesn't know what to make of this, after he is hit across the nose by a flying forearm. Mary apologizes as she follows her man around among the other dancers, trying to boogie as she goes. Rodney is a boatwright and mechanic, and a member of the Fisherman's Cooperative. He doesn't work anymore, but Mary has hope. Hilda and Alexander keep dancing with one eye on Rodney. Marvin sits back down. He was dancing alone, anyway. Wren sits for a moment looking at the playback on Emery's video camera, her hand over her mouth. "I'm sorry," she says. "Just one more song, I promise."

Someone taps Marvin on the shoulder and he turns. It's Eric Massie, an earnest young high school teacher, and an accomplished drunk. "You know," he says, "the week after they found the fella on the bridge, you know what else happened?" He pauses a moment and waits for Marvin to shrug. "Well I won't say his name, because you might know the family, but this other fella, he just went over to his aunt's house, where his aunt lived all her life, an old lady. He didn't even know her very well, because he'd been away working in Alberta for years, he just went over to her house with a gallon of gasoline, sat down on the floor in her living room, and set himself on fire. Burned himself to death right in his aunt's living room. Poor woman. She was only old, didn't know this fella who he was except he was her nephew. So that's the winter for you here in Inverness."

Marvin sees the glee on the young teacher's face as a reflection of his own abject pleasure in telling the gruesome suicide to Emery. *Schadenfreude.* He touches the young teacher's arm, and stands up. "I need another drink," he says, and heads for the bar. The pub is packed now. Marvin swerves to head out to the verandah. He doesn't feel like he needs another drink.

Alexander and Hilda stop dancing when Danny Mac-Lean leaps to the stage to thrust his fists towards the ceiling like a rock star working his fans, and he has his fans in the audience who chant "Dan-ny, Dan-ny." He grabs the mic from Molly's grip, gives her a big stage grin. She is startled but a good sport. She embraces and dances him around, kissing his neck until he breaks loose and starts to sing one of his three songs. "I'm too sexy for this song, too sexy for this song…" Rodney's spasms are re-ignited by this new energy, and he goes hurtling across the floor. His jeans are loose, and flap around his hips and threaten to slip down. His mouth flies wide open in a face as gaunt as an Edvard Munch scream. Couples flatten themselves against the walls as Mary follows, dancing and apologizing, pulling up his pants.

"He's not too bright," says someone to Alexander, meaning Danny. "He knows but three songs, and not much else. This is his glory when he comes here. He really thinks he's a rock star." Danny raises his fists again and grins triumphant at the packed stadium in his mind. He appears for his fans out of a cloud of smoke in a ring of exploding fireworks. Alexander and Hilda have had enough and go to the bar to grab their wings. They head for the verandah.

"Where are you from?" Alice grabs Mark's belt and pulls him a little closer to her table.

"Leave the fella alone," Kevin says. "Here, have a Keith's." He slides a bottle towards Marvin.

"Mind yer business. I'm doin' me own survey for the hell of it. The hello of it."

Marvin says he's from the States.

"Is that so? And how'd ya get down here?"

Marvin explains that he is staying in a friend's cabin.

"I been to Boston, that's all I been to up there. So how do ya like it down here?"

"Leave the fella alone."

"I'm doing my survey of the tourists. I want to know, does he like it?"

"I think it's very beautiful. It's a beautiful place, I think."

"There's Candy going up to sing now," Kevin says. "I bet she sings 'Sixteen Tons.' That's what she sings every time."

"It's stupid. That's a man's song," Alice says.

Hilda and Alexander step onto the verandah with their basket of chicken wings. "You know those two?" Alice asks Marvin.

"Leave the fella be."

"It's none of your business, Kevin. I'm interested." She tugs on Marvin's belt so he sits down next to her. "You just stay here one winter, shovel the snow, see how dark and cold it gets, then tell us how beautiful it is. What's your name?"

"Mark."

"Mark what?"

"Mark Allenby." His name was Allen. He didn't know why he added the extra syllable.

"Hey, you two," Alice shouts, surprising Hilda and Alexander. "What flavor of chicken wings did ya get?"

"Alice, shut the fuck up. Leave people alone."

"…and what do ya get / Another day older and deeper in debt" reverberates through the windows and the door. "She has a voice like a man," Kevin says. "It's deep."

"Ya know," Alice says, as Hilda and Alexander approach their table. They want to meet everybody, because you never know who might have a line on a great piece of property. "There are two things I really care about. You know what they are?"

"We got the spicy," Hilda says.

"Two things," Alice repeats, "I care about."

Candy gets a big round of applause for her "Sixteen Tons." Wren and Molly jump back to the microphone. "For our final performance, we're going to sing 'Bad, Bad Leroy Brown,' by Jim Croce," Molly says. "No," says Wren. "'You're So Vain,' Carly Simon. No, my mistake, Freda Payne, 'Band of Gold.'" They both look over at Elaina, and she points at the screen, then they say in unison, "'It's Raining Men,' by The Weather Girls."

"Okay," says Kevin. He is sobering up and he doesn't like it. No matter how much he drinks, at some point he starts to sober up, until he passes out. "What two things? What are the two things you care about?"

"I care about genealogy." She stares into Hilda's face as Hilda nibbles on a chicken wing. "And I love sex. I care about sex." Alexander lays an arm around Hilda's shoulder. He hasn't done that in a long time. Hilda puts a chicken wing in his mouth.

"Well that's good," Kevin says. "Then you'll always know when you're fuckin' yer brother."

Everyone at this hour is well-lubricated and raring to boogie. The young and the not so, the capable and the infirm, crowd the dance floor. Maybe the remoteness of Inverness from the centers of urban culture that produce this music gives everyone that feeling of freedom, of what-the-fuck, letting everything hang out in the brown haze of this pub. Maybe it's just the sweeter universal trips of alcohol.

Marilyn Goo-goo is sober, however, and almost leaves when she hears Elaina call her to the stage, emphasizing the name *Goo-goo*, in a way that sounds almost nasty. But she is used to it. She has found a Rita Coolidge song, and she knows what she is going to do. The only song she could find after flipping through Elaina's white pages of lists was "I'd Rather Leave While I'm In Love," a Carole Bayer Sager and Peter Allen song. That one is cued up just for her, and she is going to start singing it straight, but at a certain point she will begin a cry like the Cherokee cry that permeates Rita's *Shaman's Way* album. She will penetrate the room with a chant from her present, from her ancient ways. Why does she want to do this? She doesn't know. This is no pow-wow. There is no alcohol permitted at a pow-wow.

Marilyn watches the screen as the intro starts and the people below on the floor, who never stop dancing, are still dancing, and the bouncing ball starts to lead her through the lyric, and just as she leaves the lyric to start her chant everything goes dark—the screen, off; the sound, off; the lights, off. Silence. No clatter and whirr of the poker machines from the back. No hum of the coolers. The odor of chicken wings thickens in the atmosphere. The darkness is like stone. And outside, in the streets of Inverness, in the parking lot, not a streetlight, only a few car headlights turning pass through the window to make shadows like ghosts of the vanished dimensions.

On the verandah, conversations continue in a shifting constellation of cigarette tips.

"It's a blackout," Alexander says.

"Remember I was stuck in that elevator for four hours?" his wife says. "This is nicer. That was New York City."

"It was an hour-and-a-half, not even."

"Felt like half a day. Are there any elevators in Inverness?"

"Only in the skyscrapers, along Central Avenue. Every place else you walk up." Alice is a little impatient with the stupidity. This American is doubly in the dark, doesn't have any sense of what kind of a town is Inverness. Alice doesn't like the dark at all. "Did you get pregnant in the elevator? That's what I would have done."

"Alice, why don't you go have Gordon fix you another drink? You sound too damned sober." Kevin pushes on her.

"I'm not going in there in the dark."

Gordon scoops around with a flashlight behind the bar. He doesn't want to get too far from the cash register. He keeps

Emily with him back there, doesn't want her delivering chicken wings in the dark. So far things seem pretty calm, just the mumbling of people waiting for the lights to come back. Emily opens a few beers, one Blue for Billy Crump who sees through the window a curious glow. "Geez," he whispers. "Will you look at that, will you?" What he sees is a brightness out there over the ocean that he doesn't know how to explain. It's in the sky. The light doesn't penetrate the room, as if the window is a black screen lit up, but opaque, reflecting none of its luminescence on the interior. It seems to move in waves, and take forms. He wishes his wife had shown up to sing the Dixie Chicks, and tell him if he sees what he sees, because he sees chickens, bright chickens tumbling across the sky, a great mass of illuminated chickens is what he thinks he sees, and he's too shy to tell someone.

Edwin Frasier can't see his poker machine because the electric failure has cut it off. The frustration is that he was about to draw two cards to a flush or a possible inside straight. Just his luck. He's lost a lot of money and this win could keep him in the game. Even his wife, gone three years now, was in his mind telling him to play the hand. The darkness makes him nervous and edgy. He leaves the paddock and steps onto the verandah and up in the dimly phosphorescent sky sees a straight flush in diamonds, Queen high, pass through.

"Will you look at that? I've never seen that." Andrew is looking at the sky. To Lillian it seems as if some cosmetic cream has been spread across the firmament, a nourishing anti-wrinkle thing for the sky. Occasionally a diamond flashes. She presses herself harder against Andrew. "I like it," she says.

"I've never seen the northern lights so bright, and at the same time as the Perseid." Andrew explains it that way, but he's not sure he really knows what's going on. The electricity has failed. This he knows for sure. "We're lucky."

Lillian bites his neck lightly.

Emery chews himself out because his battery is down and he didn't bring a spare. Shit. He works in metals and wonders if he can brush aluminum to get that nacreous effect he sees through the window, and he sees, in the metallic light, form after form of possible pieces in copper, in steel or bronze, coursing through the firmament. Wren attaches herself to his arm and squeezes close as she hasn't for many years. She often uses sequins in her art strung like fractals or graphs of prime numbers or randomized constellations glittering there, and she wonders if that effect of the occasional meteor could be possible, or even desirable.

Hilda and Alexander watch as section maps one after the other, with pulsing property lines, display themselves across the heavenly vault. They have spent many days looking at maps of properties in Port Hood. "That one," Alexander whispers to Hilda.

Tessa and her mother step onto the verandah to look at the sky. "I never saw this," Tessa says. "Did you ever, mum?"

Crispi looks up and shrugs. She can think of nothing to say. It is rare that she has nothing to say. Marvin slips behind Crispi and places a hand on her shoulder. He sees the light, and finds it strange. "Do you know what this is?" he asks. Crispi turns to him, a mischievous smile on her face. "It better not be snow. If it snows in August I'm coming up to the States to live with you."

"Do you see them?" Tessa asks. She sees a stage backdrop with a whirl of ballerinas spinning past on point, or leaping into the arms of men with powerful thighs. "See what?" her mother asks. She really doesn't know how to talk about what she is seeing.

As the darkness comes, Molly is wrapped around one of the posts. She feels she has perfected her titty bar routine, and has made something different out of it, something to show her husband, Raoul, when he arrives from Pennsylvania. She sees no reason to do it in the dark. She finds her way out to the verandah, and climbs off the deck, a move that's usually against the rules, and heads past the last row of old mining company houses, through the newly planted grass, down towards the sewage treatment ponds. She flops into the grass and looks up at the bright silent splendor. *This sky is for her,* she thinks. It was her idea to advertise herself and her friend, and this was like their reward. A light perfume of processed sewage wafts across her face. The grass prickles more against her bare back than she might have expected. *The pulsing iridescence, so sexy, so silent after all the music, and the occasional rush of a meteor, also silent, is all happening for her,* she thinks. This is a signal of something in her life. She didn't expect or even want anything, but here it comes, and it is good. She closes her eyes.

When she opens, she sees, albeit dimly displayed, a panoramic Monopoly board in the sky. As the youngest of six kids in a family that played Monopoly fanatically on holidays, she started off at a disadvantage. When she closes her eyes she can see the little Monopoly man she called Mr. Pants, even before she was old enough to play. In their super-deluxe set he had striped pants, and she loved his top hat too. She often had dreams that she danced with Mr. Pants. She recognized the actual game on the board in the sky that was the first game she had ever won from her brothers and sisters. She had hotels on Park Place and Boardwalk. She held all three of the greens with three houses on each, and she had Baltic and St. Charles Place, as well as all the utilities and the railroads. Her siblings paid her and paid her. That game, she realizes, was the start of her life as a whole, confident person. She closes her eyes again. Mr. Pants is coming all the way to Canada to dance with her. She doesn't understand why she is crying. She is an artist, and maybe the tears are for the art she hasn't yet made. And here he is. "Hello, Mr. Pants," she says. *Monopoly*, she tells herself, *is not just a game. Monopoly is forever.*

Kevin stands up, his jaw slack. What he sees he has trouble believing. What he makes out is horses—fine Belgians and Percherons, Norics and Clydesdales, each of them pulling a plow across the empyrean, striating the night sky into glowing furrows. "I would do that," says Kevin. "Do what?" Alice rises and sips her vodka and cranberry. She blinks. She can't believe how the sky is unfurling in a broad tartan of light. It stretches as far and as silent as her smile.

Jamie sees something else. The whole sky-school of cod swims north before his eyes, returning themselves to the waters of the Gulf of Saint Lawrence, and to the Grand Banks. He sees this, and it is happening with little explosions in the sky, each explosion a small fishing boat casting out to drop some lines into the restored abundance.

For Gordon this is all a great pain in the arse. It is hard enough to keep the place afloat when the electricity is on, but nobody buys anything in the dark. He's almost sold out of wings, so he doesn't stand to lose much if the refrigeration is down for a long time. Warm beer is a consequence, but Hell, in a lot of places warm is how they like their beer. He's just losing money for every minute of darkness.

Emily sees the sky through the window and finds it hopeful. After the WTO protest she went with Brendan to Nevada, to the Rainbow Gathering. His head was still bandaged, but she loved being with him even better when he was hurt. It was the first time she'd been to the Rainbow Gathering, and the first time she'd taken ecstasy. The crowd was a hugging and kissing crowd. She liked it, and immediately wanted to take more X, but she didn't. When she thought about it, she didn't want to make a career of it. She keeps looking to the window, and what she sees in the sky is hope, bright hopeful tomorrows. That is where she wants to be, not behind this bar trapped in the darkness, and not even in this town where she has no more family, and has so outgrown her friends. She wants to go outside under the pearly sky of hope. Perhaps it is time to quit, maybe go up to Halifax and work there. She stoops under the counter to leave the bar and starts to work her way in the dark to the verandah. "Emily, I need you to stay here," Gordon shouts after her.

"That sounds a whole fuck of a lot better," says Cameron Fitzgerald, who has somehow worked his way to a seat on the stage, and is commencing to squawk out a slow air on his unvarnished fiddle. It makes him smile to hear its sound without amplification, without microphones.

Marilyn sees nothing out the window. Nothing shines for her as she chants in her high crying style. She doesn't mind the screeching of the fiddle beside her, because below it she can hear the singing of the drum. This is a big southern drum. It sings a deep and powerful song as it is struck by many powerful drummers. And she hears her voice multiplied around the drum as she sings an intertribal song. Her voice is a ring of singers around the drummers, and she can't see too well into the dark, but she feels the dancers and hears their ankle bells, and the clatter of shells that hang from their vests. The drum sings its song into the darkness, and she recognizes it, she remembers it. This is a song of *alsumsimkewey.*

MANIFESTO DYSFIC

fearless wordslingers! break out! flee the workshops!
make sense not! like moths in the honey jar writerlings
perform dreary veridical conventions over and again delusion
persists that the map is the territory there's gold in that there
map but a panda looms in this parking garage fixing to strip
your bamboo heart or tiger, tiger is it the lean into violence
that garments our time go have fun kiddoes thugs in our gov
con the young into war for their own craven delusions these slugs
(I mean bend over, America) (I mean who profits? Look in the bushes!)
ice sheet melt and toxic goop etcetera etcetera war profiteers
that threaten to dissolve our bindings the maimed the sick
generations of children lost to neglect and apathy
what'll we do? Describe it? Discuss it? Crazed
with recognition we have moved to detonate our revolution
with ancient new genre **DYSFIC!!!!** Our kisses cauterize
sear away descriptive, discursive formulae dead words
can never give tongue to this experience these feelings **DYSFIC** charges
language artists to emancipate language into the mystery and power
at its source in heart and cosmos the conventional assignment buries
reality in a casket of illusions **DYSFIC** is evocative, incantatory,
ecstatic not the image in the mirror nor the scene through the window
the work is to smash the mirror shatter the glass as they distort
DYSFICTIONS are anti-narrative they are dysfunctional, dysrational,
dysengaged they are politically and emotionally dyslect can be
dystasteful and **DYSFIC** is dysorderly, dyspontaneous, it is man-
ifest even though it is dysqualified and dysallowed dysprovisational

185

though in its structures it may exhibit form exquisite
as insects in a laundry often composed at randyom
DYSFICS are quick and clueless as persistently trivial as they are
relentlessly profound **DYSFIC** is always composed through a system
of exocharacterization and psychological outrisme (this doesn't mean
fuck-all, Mesdames & Monsieurs, mi dispiace) i.e., elsewhere characters
live in their books, grow, lust, murder their children, survive brutal savage
childhoods in various ethnicities, breath salt air by the shore, keep pet
alligators in the tub, fuck up the lives of their closest friends, despair of
satisfying their grandmothers, pray for a breakthrough in their diets,
conspire to sell nuclear secrets, but none of this, not a word of it,
ever manifests in a **DYSFIC** dysfictioneers grant release of brief
chuffs of steam from the eyeballs the writings resist closure, encourage
dysclosure dysfictioneers know that within every closure plumps
an efflorescence any dysclosure clears the track to THE END

DYSFICS never begin come nowhere to an ending be the perpetual
middle of things intrepidly spiritual or dyspiritual depending on field
of play you read as you do at breakfast the cereal box or casually
while you wait for the tech to come back on line or while you rest
in your attempt to get back into those tight jeans (prescribed years ago
in a different poet's manifesto) however you wiggle to compact
the flab years have wrought you'll have to face up to the **DYSFICS**
presto-chango **DYSFICTION** is right now and beyond

DYSFIC a fly on the nose of a theorist cabbage in the throat of
gender narration and bland gruel of sexual preference **DYSFIC** an ethnic
gollywobble as one of its affections **DYSFIC** embraces dyscombobulation
and silliness as no serious genre has dared and by doing thus
eliminates the pejoratives of those categories such an erasure is in the nature
of every embrace to embrace is not to embarrass we mean it we love you

186

Samuel Beckett's entreaty that we yield not to the distortions of intelligibility is proudly flown on the **DYSFIC** flag

THREE CONFLATIONS
EXTEMPORIZED

GRAMNPAD

for Ornette Coleman

Grandmothers suffer. Their daughters married in haste. The granddaughters never marry. Won't grandmothers marry again? Maybe. She scans the obituaries in the morning, and when she spots one cut loose by a dead spouse, she grabs him, i.e., a grandfather. Then the pair enters a house with heaps of comfortable shoes, crushed oatmeal boxes, moth-eaten sweaters pressed into bricks, family portraits piled up, tea cozies stuffed with petrified scones. Grandpma stack memorabilia to make a wall perforated with antique bottles. Luminousity of Coca-Cola past! It's not what they need, it's what they've used. They fill the rusting RVs of their histories with spent lightbulbs and flatten them. What a crunch, almost a noise. The grandparent of all sounds. Of this stuff they fashion a roof over the head. Don't ask how. It's a lost art. The glitz that packages our software makes excellent doors for them. They don't need to exit anyway. Not any more. Out here? In the alleged world? Why should they? The granddaughters never marry. The daughters married in haste. They shingle all this with plastic bags, thicknesses of them, so to shed the rain, and then they go in to live it out in it, i.e., life.

Whilst they complain, let them know the sun shines anyway, though maybe not so amiably as when they once enjoyed it, but it shines down these days. If they complain, tell them the dogs bite, and the bite is worse than the bark. When they complain, treat them to a meal deal. Take them fishwiches and double Big Macs. Ply them with elevator music. Take them suits of polyester. Take them mairzy doats, and doazy doats. Take them an electronic brain. Ask them to show off the Lindy Hop, even the Mashed Potato. Take them a rasher of plutonium. Take them Wittgenstein, Einstein, Gertrude Stein. Take them science and philosophy, heaps of it. Take them Whitehead and Russell. Remind them of Santayana. Make them shoot hoops. Make them play big time. Take them Miltown and Prozac and etcetera. Ragg Mopp. Take them a red-nosed reindeer.

All the delights of their own devising, take them. Take them Elvis Presley in the form of an oral vaccine. Tell them life is as good as what you make of it. Take them color television when they complain. Take them Carmen Basilio. Take them Alfred E. Newman. Take them Jimmy Rodgers.

Jean Seberg gazes into the rooms where her grandchildren entertain their guests. In one room Baudry has set up a small theater, three rows, five seats to a row, and there he screens for three of his friends, aficionados of the cinema, herself starring in *Breathless*, then appearing as Joan of Arc, being burned, actually burned at the stake by Otto Preminger, who got what he wanted out of his actresses, then in *Paint Your Wagon*, pretty as a Hollywood babe. They watch these movies late into the night, their eyes reddened, tearing. One might think they were weeping. *Wipe your tears,* Jean Seberg thought to say. *Don't cry for me.* Then she thought, *Why not let them cry? I was beautiful, and mine was the saddest story.*

Thelin, in another room, reads to his wife and a couple they met on a cruise to Iceland. The text is Jean Seberg's deposition at the FBI hearings on the Black Panther Party. Although

THREE CONFLATIONS EXTEMPORIZED

the other husband has fallen deep into the velour asleep, it is evident from the expression on the face of the two women that they are moved, even shocked. *Don't be so surprised,* she wants to say. *It could happen to you. Just expose your upraised palms once to the winds that fly from these buildings.* But she doesn't say it. This is not her voice.

Mercurey in the third room is undressing for her lover. That lover is one of the many lost granddaughters of Alice B. Toklas. How can they be lost? Jean Seberg doesn't know what to say to this. She wants to sing, maybe. She wants to understand everything. She can't resist peeping.

"I had no children," Jean Seberg asserts. "The grandchildren are an illusion, and they never marry. I am an illusory grandma, and my illusory daughters married in haste."

"Furthermore, I am dead," she pleads.

Grandmothers have conditions. Grandmothers sing the blues. Grandmothers wake up. Grandmothers in poverty. Grandmothers ethnic roots. Grandmothers in the home towns. Grandmothers splitting rocks. Grandmothers queer. Grandmothers beat the odds. Grandmothers control the guns. Grandmothers fly the Concorde. Grandmothers know the score. Grandmothers on their skateboards. Grandmothers excellent. Grandmothers have a heart. Grandmothers pickling. Grandmothers hello. Grandmothers of the flesh. Grandmothers concentrate. Grandmothers run the country. Grandmothers down and out. Grandmothers turn technical. Grandmothers to the wall. Grandmothers take no shit. Grandmothers never yield. Grandmothers on the run. Grandmothers with the answers. Grandmothers at the barricades. Grandmothers smoke opium. Grandmothers make yogurt. Grandmothers on Harleys. Grandmothers take a beating. Grandmothers back at seven.

Grandfathers, on the other hand, doze off while watching the store. Around them the predators fly in a circle of bliss. From the grandfathers they can extract a bitter that inculcates a sense of life into those grandchildren who have failed as mates. They know, as grandfathers do, that life is less important; but a sense of life is everything.

SWATORRE

for Steve Lacy

*sick juice blues   no clean greens   big bomb charm   crush
cups cupboards blow house   sleep down dreams   monkey poison person   chicken no more scratch   chicken
sickens   big beef eruption   fluck   the nurse be killer
mole meat me   roll tanks on you   mosquito dreams blow
truck   nuck*

    –Hey, sis. Selling any anthrax?

    –Come again. What?

    –You heard me. Anthrax. I've got you for exchange one
fresh kidney, from a white man. But don't try to give none of
that animal vaccine crap; I want the military grade. I'm educated in this shit.

    –Let's see. All I've got left now is some bubonic. That's it.

    –I don't use the bubonic. I need anthrax. I been to your
store before.

    –How long can you wait?

    –What does it take?

    –Three weeks, at least. This *materiel* does not grow on
trees.

    –I know what it is. Just make it swift. Too much crap going
on downtown; makes us edgy. Kids in perambulators. Jugglers
on bikes. Tall people. Short people. We need to terminate.

—I'll do what I can, okay. And if you throw in a liver, I'll put some bubonic on for free.
—The anthrax is what makes the deal. Big hurry, too. A lid buys you one kid. Lid-and-a-half gets you the whole sweet pair. But I can't deal with bubonic. It spoils.
—You get yourself a flash freezer. Bubonic keeps in the freezer compartment.
—Yeah. When you defrost you've got ring-around-the-rosie. It's Buboes in the brains, man. Like a hooker's douche-water in there, pardon my French. I don't have funds for new equipment, thank you very much. Listen, I'm tellin' you this. These kidneys are so fresh your baby sucks them, guaranteed from a white man, a young Caucasian youth. Smell like lilacs in May. Get a certain quantity of the anthrax to me by tomorrow and you can have the whole kit. Heart and lungs too.
—Okay, I can work on it; but something else, and don't take this personal, but we don't take the organs from a man. The ladies won't tolerate the male organs.
—I'm holding a truckload, sis. You can grab whatever you like, gender-specific.

dead beans bagels dead beasts   ride the crumb wagon you don't get to the feast beelzeboobs   richard degrate nailed in a crate   the tanks are coming the tanks are coming   me-hopes in a pinch to be buying the helicopter   hoops dance no more   baby crush crush baby   increase a crease add grease click salvation wonton toxicity   who owns this fuck-in planet   big city jews bombs away blues irrelevance of the occupants   china blues india blues paki blues bali blues yugo smash albania add greece   jew smash arab smash jew and hindoo smash muslim smash hindoo   let's talk economics now   baghdad smash dc not likely dc smash grenada smash panama smasha bagadadda   speak to us noriega   havana no smash nobody   cigar wars not our wars   swat iraq swat korea not swat china swat tibet

—How much you get for gas?

—How much you got?

—I give you some lungs.

—More than that.

—I give you the eyes too, my two good eyes for looking out onto the variable expanses, or into the books and on the screens and fair countenance of sons and daughters I give.

—Not *basta*.

—Okay my eyes my lungs the fair countenances my daughter's skin and ovaries.

—More.

—Okay. Eyes, lungs, fair countenances, daughter's skin and ovaries, testicles of the son, and my complete whole wife, and my plantation, and my gay caballero.

—Closer, but not enough.

—Okay. My eyes, my lungs, the fair countenances, my daughter's skin and ovaries, some testicles, my complete wife, my plantation, my gay caballero. The town I own and love by right of birth and all the people in the town I own—they live there and I roll them into no fault asphalt—and the view of the sweet blue air and the taste of the morning and rosy smudges of early light on our snow-capped mountains and the shining sea and the smell of snow and my country, my whole country and row upon row of pretty maids all in a row and the golden years and the smell of snow again.

—Alright. But I have the option to take more, push comes to shove; in the meanwhile, I don't know why I'm being so generous. You get three gallons for that, and I toss in an additional imperial quart, no extra charge.

the whale fails   punch punch judy judy punch punch pinch owl   certain owls gone forever certain salamanders finished   finnegan's warbler never exists yet six legs on certain frogs   condor creeps away

–I'm gonna do it.

–Do what?

–I'm gonna conduct my own first underground nuclear test. I'm definitely gonna conduct it.

–Get outta here.

–It's the first test of its kind by a private citizen, conducted by one.

–That just doesn't sound like something a woman would do. Not some woman I'd want to know.

–Well you already know me, dip-hands; I've got the hole mostly dug, already, and I got the nuke on order; at least, I know where to get it. See how much you know about women?

–Where do you order a nuke for yourself?

–I don't think I can tell you yet. Maybe I'll tell you after.

–What good is this gonna do? Why do you want to do this?

–I'm about to be the first private citizen to demonstrate nuclear capability as a woman. This is going to make a difference. How good are you with a shovel?

–I don't know. This gives me a lot to think about.

–Since when do real men think? Only kidding. Only joshing.

A HUMBLE SUGGESTION

It being well known that conflicts arise in the course of human events that are pursued zealously into action by one and then the other faction, and that these actions result frequently in the production of many tons of human carcass, sometimes in great heaps that heretofore have been disposed of en masse, or hidden and denied in such a way that these mass interments have come to be viewed by ourselves as a great waste of human resource, and in recognition of the fact that the condition of many of those not yet directly affected by these conflictions is for the great part one of deprivation, poverty, starvation, and offering the possibility that we have the will and the technology to affect this situation, we make the following suggestion to those with the power to effectuate such development and change.

We are prepared to establish an organization mobilized to act in situations such as those described above, as well as any other that might eventuate to profit our intentions, such as the common genocide, guerrilla war, cult suicide, air disaster or mudslide, tsunami, postal massacre, schoolboy rampage, ecological reversal, and et cetera and et cetera; we will be prepared to service whatever occurrences might eventuate to interrupt the natural course of human experience and turn significant quantities of fresh human remains into fresh meat; we are prepared to process as few as ten, and as many thousands as will be available. We propose to be present to help any of those who find they've escaped from and are untouched physically by any so-called calamity, to nourish themselves, improve themselves, even prosper through their position outside the abiding pandemonium.

To this end we offer our expertise in the arts of dressing, carving, preserving, packaging, provisioning, and distributing. We propose to bring into operation the newly outfitted mobile meat dressing plants we have developed and installed in recycled postal vehicles, school buses, and tour buses. The largest of these mobile plants have the capacity to strip from the bone, dress, cut up, package, and refrigerate or freeze the edible portions of ten or more carcasses every half-hour. Using these flexible instruments in the field we will have the capacity to respond to situations almost as soon as they happen, much as does the international press; in fact, we expect to cooperate with the media, sharing information so that each agency can arrive at a scene of production expeditiously, while the matter is still fresh. We hope that as such events are planned by factions in conflict we will have instilled enough confidence in the various parties that they will not hesitate to contact us as soon as they determine to carry out events appropriate to our mission. We hope to function out of neutrality and humanity, much as does the Red Cross or the Red Crescent.

–How do you know when one of these is dead?

–I like to kick it, and if it doesn't moan or wiggle that's enough to assume.

–What about brain dead?

–That's a given. I can't worry about that. As far as I'm concerned you're brain dead unless you show me different.

Many of our operators have been well trained, are former employees of Swift and Company, and among them a goodly number express interest in training other citizens to perform these acts of conservation when the number of carcasses is too small for our machines to process efficiently. Packages of these comestibles can be distributed effectively through various food share programs, once the stigma against the nutriment is dissipated. We should be able to educate the people to this, through slogans, and through an appeal to the common sense of most good citizens in need. The meat is not unpalatable when flavored; much like pork, it is said, though some compare it to turkey; and through repeated exposure many will likely develop a taste for the product. It can be sold cheaply in stores in frozen ten-pound bricks, and the income from this commodity used to repair infrastructure that invariably suffers while this foodstuff is being created.

–Okay, first let me ask you what you're looking for yield-wise. Kilotons? Megatons?

–Why not? A good yield is good, right?

–Lady, I look at you and I want to give you the benefit of my experience. You're like a newcomer, is it not? Yield is like size, like it isn't necessarily size that counts. Am I right? I mean about size.

–Well, size…

–When I first got into this business, it was about five billion per device, and the yield was tiny by present standards. That's when they were building "fatman," "trinity," "little boy," "number four," that series. Hey, wait a minute, come to think of it "number four" is still available. You could get it bargain basement. Still in the crate. Depends on what your purpose is,

if you can go with a smaller yield. They would love to recover
some of that R&D money. It's got collector's value. That could
be a nice unit for you, as a thing to have around as an antique,
maybe. You could keep it somewhere, show it off. But if you
need to use it, you know; with a thing like this, you use it you
lose it. Like poof, KABAAM. That's the downside of this kind
of collection.

—My purpose is, as an individual citizen, and as a woman,
it's to explode the first citizen initiated—

—I'm all for it, okay. Depends on what you're looking for,
quantity-wise. You want some B61s, we've got a few available.
Or there's a box of W78s, wrapped and ready to go. A short
wait for the W80-1s, and the B61-11s. Scads of B83s, if that's
what you're looking for.

—Well, I was just thinking one was all I need.

—One?

—To start with.

—I could have stayed in bed for one. That's like asking for
one peanut.

—How many do you think I need?

—Wait. Let's approach it this way. What are you looking at
for a delivery system? Have you thought that one over yet?

—Well, my plan is to...

—Hold on. Let me pitch this for you first. What I'd like to
involve you in is a B-2A Spirit, at two-point-six-billion a copy,
and it's worth every dollar you spend over the B52H, even if at
list that looks good for 42.9 mill. a pop. No muss no fuss with the
Spirit. You maybe don't have aeronautical skills, so you might
have to hire a pilot; that's all, as far as crew. With the B52H
you'll have a payroll. Realistically you could fly this Spirit thing
yourself, lady. It's like your boudoir in the sky.

—I'm going to do it underground. We're preparing the hole myself. I intend to produce here the first underground nuclear test conducted by a private citizen, who is a woman. That's what I want you to understand. I'm doing this as a woman.

—Attagirl. I'm all for it, whatever you want to do, but let me see if I can raise for you another option, another way to think about it. Have you ever thought underwater? It's much more feminine, like a water ballet thing. I'll tell you, for a limited time I've got a price on a sweet boat for you, a submarine, Trident, Ohio-class. Completely armed for four billion plus or minus. You can do what you want with it. I'm assuming you're a U.S. citizen.

—Right now, one device. One thing, that's what I want to do.

—Sweetie, I can't talk just one device. If I could, I would; but I put together packages. I'm not in a retail business. I hate to disappoint a sweetheart like yourself, so what I'm going to do, and I might get shot down for this, is give you the name of a friend of mine at Whiteman in Missouri. Even with him it would be a lot easier to talk if you want quantity, but he's done single items before, you know, for idealistic reasons. You've got the talent to convince him this is a good cause. Guy's got a heart. So I can't give you a price on what one of his beauties goes for, retail; but he'll want his cash in advance, and it's a different business he does. He won't deliver. You'll have to pick it up. He drops it off a truck into a ditch by the road, and you've got to be there quick, to grab it out of the ditch.

A HUMBLE SUGGESTION : CONCLUSION

There could well be corollary psychological benefits to this practice we propose, some improvement that might soon be seen in the spirits of the people constrained to effectuate the activity that creates our product. These are mostly men who see themselves as having no choice in the matter, and know that historically such events are inevitable as the culling of the herd, if one were to go so far as to husband one's peers as he would dumb beasts; yet there is much pressure on them to suffer recriminations and feel guilt for what they do. Why should they feel guilty, if they are doing what will inevitably be done? Making their efforts through our auspices result in a product of great benefit to the many who are in need will do much to alleviate whatever loss of morale occurs in the ranks of those performing the inevitable. A general upliftedness could be the result, a great sunrise over what once was called merely a killing field. I can't but think of the difference we might have made in Cambodia, in Vietnam, in Rwanda, and looking back into dimmer histories, if we followed the Turks into Armenia, if we could have been at Wounded Knee, or with the charges of King Leopold in the Congo. You could utilize us in Afghanistan. Please consider our services in Iraq, maybe Korea, could be Kashmir. We are totally mobile. When we consider the healthier and more profitable outcomes that could have followed the Germans through their Holocaust had our technology been practical at the time, it makes us weep, makes us almost weep.

BUTSTTS

for Cecil Taylor

In the sunlight at the edge of the crowd a great hound lay kerchiefed in rayon. The snug delta-winged aircraft circled low as if this were an aerodrome of the other kind. As it left the service elevator the big hawk stretched its wings, drying them in the sun, then looked over what had come to be known as "the situation." Alack, alas. Swift as a nude bather, he tunneled beneath the gathering to emerge by a bench six hundred feet from the faded hound. That was the hawk and that was the hound, sing fol de rol, fol de lay, fol de fol fol. As if this were an aerodrome of the other kind the snug delta-winged flying apparatus circled low. Butts of an uncertain ilk dropped from the sky like plushy mosses—sphagnum, purslane, even Irish, or like exotic bromeliads like pineapples and Spanish moss, harbingers of the coming gods. Were the gods coming? Rickety Buckets elucidated, "My enema is not your enemy, Alfred." Excusing himself, Herman rattled over to the liberation pulpit. "Let there be drunks!" The hawk, a fallow female of the elevator-riding species, *Buteo Ascensoria*, recognized Herman immediately as her liege and lumbered towards him. "The hound is autistic, that one swaddled in rayon," was how she greeted Herman, who ignored this, but then spotted the dog and rushed across the sward to dive straight out and land full-belly-down-flat on the kerchiefed flank. "Woof," from the hound. In the creature's mind were the complete names and the contents of every meal ever eaten by every person ever to live in every apartment at 43 Crosby Street, a twelve-story high-rise with one hundred and eight units. But the poor hound had no way to express this information in the language of humans. O idiots savant, awack, awass. Circling low over the situation as if it were an aerodrome of the other kind, a snug delta-winged flying contraption kept dropping butts. "Nice butts," said Herman. "No ifs or ands about them." This was in the future. Today we'll hear a different story.

The effervescent Rastafarian shoe designer, Tobias I. Nix, stepped onto his balcony and looked askance. Down there the footprints of five avenging angels were palpable even through the crowd that had gathered across the turf. The surrounding folks were thick as marshmallows in a blue box, but not so opaque. Those footprints showed through like testicles in Ziploc bags. GLAD Bags. Two terrifying angels still were unaccounted for. "Alfred," the shoe designer exclaimed, "the preparations!" The mob separated to allow the serpent, who before it arrived had been announced as a battery-powered tongue, to levitate and then penetrate the snugly slung, delta-winged airship that circled, looking for a better aerodrome. "Wheest groose!" the delta-wing exclaimed as it suffered the violation. Rickety Buckets elucidated. "Wheest is the yeast, but groose is not gross." Margot Margolies' mother mollified the multitude. That was in the future. Now, the following:

Spicy aromas of spargic acid blew across the green. Finally, asparagus season. At this time of year the congregation turned Herman loose from his diurnal burdens so he might apostrophize, lecture, preach, or what-have-you to the acres upon miles of tender spears erecting through the sod in anticipation of sauces or vintage balsamic vinegar. Some awaited the summer with apprehension. The revolution was kinking in. Soon some shooting would begin. Why not? Wouldn't you? Aren't you one of the oppressed? You are a minority, or a female of your species, is it not? The oppression is heavy, the poverty deep, the suffering unimaginable. And isn't "the situation" deteriorating, and won't you be the one to suffer more? You and yours? Them and theirs? Rickety Buckets elucidated, "News cannot be always new, but it can be noose." Tobias Nix felt the trouble coming, though he didn't believe in trouble, not really, not trouble. "Alfred," he whispered plaintively, "the preparations!" Alfred was busy, chatting up the two avenging angels that remained outside the napping crowd. "We've got the money," they said, as if they were one angel. "And you need the backing." The sounds of war blew in from the distance. Alfred gazed at his effervescent shoe designer, Tobias I. Nix, a man who counted on him when stuff started to move, like blood on its clots. Can these avenging angels be trusted? Nix shook his head. What a bright head, big as a tuba. Maybe this was the earthquake, maybe a parade. It could be the biggest one of all time. This was overdue—for the earth to crack in two. The snug delta-winged aircraft held its position as the lawn below turned slowly on a pivot, as if it were trying to be the aerodrome of the other kind, some kind of turntable operative, something beyond the ordinary, a special kind of strip. How many were involved by now? How many dead? All of them? Was everybody happy? How many were fooling themselves? All of them, fooling all of us. All of them! All of us! Asparagus pushed up like some loopy phalloids. Why not? Butts landed on their tips. Big butts. This was in the future. Today we hear another story.

"Reggae is the past, admittedly a greater past," Rickety Buckets elucidated. "But the past is overcooked. The past is not pasta." In our times the trivial is typical, and the typical is not what we need. A return to beyond the boring is needed. Perhaps a nasty hawk, and a hound that once smoked Lucky Strikes, sing fol de rol, fol de lay, fol de fol fol. Victims lay in the midst, and in the sunlight survivors from the edge slowly sifted in to look for loved ones. Only loved ones had died. This is the story. If you are not loved, you will tend to live this way. A grey pall had settled on the mall, so one could hardly see the violated delta-winged aircraft circling low, over this aerodrome of the other kind. But we could smell it, and it smelled like cusps. Alfred lifted the pitiful hound onto his back and returned to Warsaw. "Without shoes?" Tobias I. Nix worried, "and no preparations."

"What is good for the hound," Herman said, lifting his arms in a celebration of times gone by. "Times don't go by," Rickety Buckets countered. "It is ourselves going by and by and by. Times is a cyclical unit and we only appear to undulate on its printout like a disappearing script." A palimpsest? That's us! Now Rickety Buckets is running for office. "Office and coffin are close," he elucidates. "I've got the shoes, but where are the women?" Tobias I. Nix complains. Now the parade begins. Today the story is different. Now is the future. Today the story is different.

Abby builds her deck. Betsy wins the argument. Connie files the papers. Dolores masters golf. Eleanora starts a riot. Florence takes her triplets to the zoo. Gertrude blows it. Helga needs one more dog. Ida sits on the still. Jackie berates. Karin makes a go of it. Linda gives us more than something extra. Marian picks up the trombone. Nikki pumps iron. Olivia wants absolute victory. Patsy has already got the future figured out. Queenie lives from day to day. Rowena presides. Samantha is Miss Origami. Tabatha has the mind of a mechanic. Ulrika waits 'til the time is right. Vivian has perfect pitch. Wanda has perfect aim. Xenia has a perfect mind, but shyly. Yolanda always grabs the bull by the horns. Zelda collapses the contraption. Zora rubs a smudge. Yaphia pilots airships. Xaviera retools. Wilhemina emits rays. Vanna swipes whiskey. Undine divorces. Tanya edges closer. Sybil holds a flush in clubs. Rachel writes the best novel. Quinta makes the chorus work. Penny beats the bushes. Oona obsesses. Nelly unlocks the library. Maureen harbors a grudge. Lucille takes control. Kim finishes the woodwork. Janet ups the ante. Isadora installs a shower filter. Harriet designs the bridge. Gail weighs her boyfriends. Fanny makes the Supreme Court. Esther hefts the newsy's pistol. Diana ships vegetables. Corinna goes ballistic. Barbara solos Boston to Beirut. Alison finds the glitch.

As the rest are watching.

This is in the future.

The busts fall from an airship, and land with some thumps. It was a blimp to be exact, that inadvertently crosses the divide and finishes under the bridge that separates A from B. All through the day they fall and fall, all of them falling, o fall de rall, fall de lley, fall de fall fall. The women from A quickly fabricate the pedestals and ship them to B. Displayed on their pedestals these fallen busts promote a season of optimism and dread. Such a drift can free any hound from rayon and open each elevator to its hawk. Oh, the change seasons. Ouch! Does so-and-so happen? The story remains to be told. A blimp can hover, or it can move, slowly, as it prefers; or rather, as its pilot prefers. She is Margot (the merry) Magnolo, in charge. This is in the present. This is right now. Music so melancholy. Cruelty so extreme. Rescue so complete. Yesterday was on its way.

No more will be described.

The next day comes.

PARROTS IN CAPTIVITY

(IN CAPTIVITY)

...the words of the parrot
is the noise of silence...

—*Melinda Dixon*

Monday morning again, and the packaged crackers are in revolt. They snapped from their wrappers while I was meditating, and now they're airborne, crumbs of Triscuits and grahams and rye crisps, making a regular pollution of the air in the loft. I'm not used to this. The Ritzies hover in the skylight, releasing a fine rain of palm oil and salt.

"Those crackers give me the creeps." Andrew, my parrot, sharpens his beak on his perch. "I'm not of the hummingbird species. Nor am I any kind of a bat. I am so merely parrot."

"Not so merely," I squawk.

Ilyana enters, headed for work. She kicks through the Styrofoam peanuts, the packing boxes, and the bubble wrap that clutter our loft, while giving it a spirit of life on the go, though if either of us could figure out how, decide when to do it, we would discard all this *materiel*. Neatness takes courage and stealth.

"I didn't know you were getting up so early," I tell her. We live together, but she has her own place elsewhere, just in case.

She ignores me. All three of her pagers are paging, and two of her cell phones ring. She drops a sheet of paper between my legs as she passes my cushion. She kneels by the stereo and ignites the CD player. Andrew has taken wing. A gray feather rides a slant of late winter light that bangs in through a high window. Ilyana slides her super slim hand into the CD slot, and a green mustard glow worms through the veins of her wrist. I look over the sheet of paper she so fliply flipped at me. It is dated March 8, and titled FOR ANDREW IN CASE OF WAR OR ANY CONDITIONS OTHERWISE PERTAINING. Andrew is my name, as it is the name of this parrot.

Dear Andrew,
No more tic the nippies; no more heft the booblet.

(*Booblet*, indeed. *Tic the nippies*, indeed. She tends to the *prezioso* sometimes)

No more tongue to cock tip, no more lip the balls.
No more sit on face; no more stiff in bung.
No more sphincter licking; no more nose the clit.
No more slide on thick joint; no digits in wet gush.
No more juice and jigs; no pipping at the perineum.

(*Pipping at the Perineum*, sounds Big Band)

No more nothing. Stop. No war. Stop. No more. Stop. Stop.

Ilyana loves to make the rules, and so doing gets a little gross, thank God. What terrifies her about the War, any war, this war—that someone else makes ALL the rules.

"My rules make the world spacey and inhabitable, and more...sexy," is what she says. She breaks the rules too.

"Nothing else in the world, no feeling as good as this feeling," she sings now into the crumb-packed air. She means the feeling of her hand plugged into the CD slot. I never saw anyone do that before. I'm kind of itching to try it for myself.

"Don't you answer your pagers?"

Her head bends back on her pale latte neck, the gaze floating up to the skylight. "Look, Andrew. Look up there."

My thought is that she's just avoiding her pagers, avoiding my question; but, not so. She sees something. There is a *quelque-chose* disturbing the manifestation of crumbs in the skylight. This parrot is all grabs—beak and talons, snatching the Wheat Thin militants out of plain air.

"Andrew," I cry up to where he flaps in the cracker chaos, a whir of wings, as if he were the world's largest example of its smallest bird. Kamikaze crackers dive at him from every angle. Not even the hairiest saltine, nor the nimblest Waverly Wafer can avoid the lightning of his grab.

"I never thought I could do this, Andrew," he mumbles, beak full of what-polly-wants. "But I was perched there in a quandary, saying to myself, *Andrew, you good for nothing parrot guy, what the hell are you doing with your life? It's crisis time.* So just like that I went for it. And you know what? I can do it. I've got the right stuff. Andrew, my man, I'm a goddamned helicopter of redemption."

Andrew is an African Grey parrot, a species with an unlimited vocabulary. Although the debate is on about whether you can attribute cognition to these birds, I don't care. Andrew's example gives me courage to rise from my cushion, to abandon my meditation. Don't hurl, my brothers and sisters, when I ask you to understand that meditation is my crackers, my hand in the CD slot. Meditation is my personal feedlot in the whole garbage-y world, my peaceful cranny against the wars current or impending. I approach Ilyana, waving her paper in front of myself.

"You made up these rules? This is modus vivendi for us?"

She exits her hand from the slot and lifts it as a scepter between us, the glowing trowel of our separation. I am moved to explain how much I love her, but her chuckling pagers push me back. Who knows how many lovers at this moment are aching to get in touch?

"Don't jump to conclusions, Andrew. What you have there is my poem, one from my HIV and anti-war sequence. I made this for the NEA. It's in a form I invented, called the Rumcroft." She flicks the page with her forefinger. "My poems have their own rules."

"So what is it? Are you afraid of getting HIV? Getting it from me?"

She stretches long as her six-foot-four slender body will extend. The pale brown of her face is crossed by blue shadows from the skylight, and as she turns the shallow hammocks scooped between her clavicles and shoulders fill with darkness. "I'm a woman, Andrew. W-O-M-Y-N. I don't fear anything from you."

"Damn, Ilyana. Do you know how much I love you?" It's a relief to say it. I want to keep saying it, now.

"Why. Because I have no fear? You love my big shoulders?"

"I love love love love love love you. You."

"There is one thing I am afraid of, come to think of it, that I can catch from you." She holds the hand, still glowing, in front of her face.

"What are you afraid of catching from me?"

"War," she breathes, with her fuck-me sensuality. "The disease men spread like a plague of warts." She lowers the hand. Her face glows.

I look away. My voice is enfeebled by what she has just said. "I love looking at you. I hunt for your spine, your unpredictable heart, Ilyana." I slap the sheet of paper. "And you keep us organized." This is the kind of conversation it's best to finish expeditiously. "Do you love me, Ilyana?"

"Of course." Andrew swoops into the last cracker enclave. "I love a man who nurtures a parrot."

Today I have my appointment with the President of the United States of America, though he is perhaps too busy promoting various agendas—his war, for instance—to take time for my issues.

Andrew loves to watch me dress for such engagements, and registers with a squawk how I like to slink into my three-thousand thread count Egyptian cotton dress shirt, deep burgundy, feel it slip over my torso, a near zero friction coefficient, slipperier than silk. A pale lime double-breasted pin-stripe Armani suite closes over my dusty pink velour tie, and my feet in evening blue socks hidden by gray suede high-top Vans sneakers.

Andrew swoops to my shoulder. "Looking sharp, Andrew."

I push him away, to one of his perches.

"You tell the president not to blast Iraq so much with his technologically advanced boom-booms. He kills too many parrots."

"Those are people, Andrew."

"God is a parrot. You tell that to the president."

I open the elevator door.

"You live in a big loft on the top floor. You got the privileges, *vato*. You got all the luxuries."

"So what?" I ask as I step into the elevator. As if I have to ask him anything.

"You bring in *mucho dinero*, Conchito." His previous owner was a Puerto Rican Romilar queen, who died in a sex shop shootout.

The wind is cold and lifts a layer of street grime into the air. Airborne are several pages of the newspapers, headlines heralding something or other about the unnecessary war foisted by a self-serving cabal, with no flexibility or imagination. I hope this president hasn't decided to protect me, because that could be a death sentence. At one time when the wind was full of this kind of grime and dust, I would cover my mouth so as not to breathe it in, but since the World Trade Center was laid waste I take it into my lungs, because this dust is a taste of my friends—nice Henry with his head full of hockey stats, Sophia with the sultry voice, Charles the compassionate, Mustafa the nervous atheist, dark Lily and Marcus the secretive—who surely still make up some of the dust in the air, and I refuse to deny them, or anyone else lost in the catastrophe, entry to my body, protection of my blood. I shall perpetuate their minced vestiges.

The cardboard sign of the victim camped in the next doorway has blown over. I stand it back up and secure it with a block of wood. He has printed it in an impressive calligraphy, with a magic marker.

PLEASE HELP
I WANT TO FIGHT FOR MY COUNTRY   I AM DYING OF AIDS
MY FAMILY HAS ABANDONED ME   I AM THE ENEMY OF
ALL THE ENEMIES OF MY COUNTRY   MY FRIENDS HAVE
LEFT ME   AGENCIES REFUSE MY CASE BECAUSE I AM A
JUNKY   I WILL KILL FOR MY COUNTRY   I WILL PROTECT
AND SERVE   I HAVE NO HOPE AND I HAVE NO MONEY
PLEASE HELP

As I have every day since he showed up a week or so ago, I put a dollar in his cup. He lets out a small squeak of thanks, and a line of spittle comes to his cracked, bloody lips. I bend a bit closer to listen to him better. His face is blotched with exposure and disease. The last sweats of dying reek from him. His piss and excrement smell sweet by comparison. A skinny arm, covered with lesions, twists out of the pile of rags and reaches for my face. He says something. I get closer. "What?" I ask. "Kiss me," he says. "Please kiss me." His pucker is a coiled snake, his tongue a molten spoon. Immediately I straighten up. This is the way it is.

A cab runs me uptown.

We get closer to my office, near the museum, where the density of homeless and derelict seems to diminish, or at least get absorbed into the crowds of people more like myself, the kind of people who make the money. They walk to their businesses in their thick overcoats, locked dispatch cases strapped to their wrists. Everything leads to my meeting with the president. I don't look forward to it, but neither do I dread it. What I have to say to him I can't say to anyone else.

My tongue grazes my lips. Though they never touched his, my lips taste of the dying man. Now that I have almost tasted death, I am sure of death. The rest of my life will be a long process leading there. Death, death, death. Sweet. As a word it's more soothing than *money*. Maybe death is a renovation, a trip to the body shop. Perhaps the president will know. In the first place, I never requested its opposite. I never said to mommy, daddy, "Let me have life!" For anyone who does life, death always follows. The newspapers fill with it, never enough. The president promises a hatful of death as his war-wish comes true. I once thought death was a semi coming at me in reverse.

219

But now they tell me that death is like corn on the cob, or cous-cous on a bun. I don't mean to get silly. I love corn on the cob. Daredevil couriers graze by on sleek bicycles, their packs slung across one shoulder, full of numbers that turn business in the city. The air around the buildings is full of numbers. Numbers rain down from the skyscrapers. I pay the cabby a number of dollars, and walk to my building across from the museum. There is little time to waste. I am later than usual, but still anticipate my encounter with the man who for the last year has lived under the arch of the shallow colonnade of the church. "I'm an artist," he always says, "can you help me out till my next show?" He is able to hollow his hand into a substantial bowl. "I used to live in a tent in the park, but they tossed us all, ya know. The president won't let us back in."

I often mention to him that I once was an artist, thinking to engage him in a conversation, but he won't be swayed from his routine.

"A dollar, or whatever you got lying at the bottom of your pocket, that's all," he repeats. And when he gets it he says, "Thank you, sir. You've helped a starving artist. Joy to you."

He's not out on the street today, but I see him crouched inside the colonnade, holding a sandwich to his mouth, his hands in grey gloves, fingers cut at the first joint, body bent as if to hide under a tent of greasy blankets. I approach him there with a dollar held out in my hand. This has been the toll I have paid for months now, to cross the street. He doesn't reach for it, but looks at me through pale brown eyes, a delirium of disappointment.

"I can't take it," he says.

"It's a dollar for a starving artist." I hope he doesn't think I'm trying to mock his routine.

"Come back later. I can't take it now. I'm on my lunch break."

I look at my watch. I don't know what to say, except, "It's not even eleven o'clock, and you're already on break?"

"If you think this isn't work, you try it some time. I do a day's work here. I was up and at 'em early. You run your business, and I'll run mine. Right now I'm closed."

I feel uncomfortable holding out the dollar, so I lay it on the pavement at his feet. He shrinks away.

"Look, can't you help me out," I say. "I've got to get across the street, and every day it costs me a dollar. Help me out. Take the dollar so I can get to work."

"What you got to do today?"

"Today I see the president."

He grins, exposing the egg salad that covers his teeth. "You full of shit too, man."

"Look at all those lights in the Trump Tower. Deals are being finalized while I stand here."

He inflates his cheeks and waves his head from side to side.

"Look," I say, "I used to be an artist."

His laugh sprays egg flecks on my wing-tipped sneakers. "And a Gulf War or so ago I used to be in Special Forces, a nasty motherfucker. I'm still nasty."

"Take the dollar."

"What time is it?"

"Twenty to eleven."

"Okay, Mr. Used-to-be-an-artist. Leave it here. If it's still here in twenty minutes, after I'm done with my lunch, call it even. If it's gone, then tomorrow is a two buck trip."

A squad car pulls up to the curb. The cops within squint

at my man. "Let him be, he's my brother," I say. "I'll take care of him when I leave the office."

In size, my office is not so impressive, a modest room on the forty-third floor in suite 4343. Several small businesses have taken rooms in this suite, and we pool our resources to pay Hilda, the receptionist, who sits at the desk in the entry to take messages and greet clients. She hardly looks up from her book, *Jude the Obscure*, which she has been reading for more than a year; not even when I tell her that I am expecting the president. Of course, I am also anticipating a trip to D.C., or to Dallas, if it turns out to be necessary. Maybe in those cities this war makes sense.

Even in this suite of offices, I am not a big player, not like Duncan & Weist in rooms twelve to sixteen, who are hanging on now in commodities and junk bonds. My small office has its desk, a couple of chairs, a leather couch. It has framed prints from the museum shop at street level across the way. I am a member of that museum, a member for life. Many of its other members are dead. Death is a member of that museum. When I was an artist, I expected my own works to be on display there one day. I can't say I ever got to do anything I can call my own work. At least the money I have, what's left of it, is my own. I was happy to discover the nature of money. It's not currency. Art is currency, and some of the artists use it to pay the bills. Money, on the other hand, is a virus, variable in its effects, that spreads through the cables, telephone, optical, and now, sometimes, wireless.

I trap the virus on my flat-screens, watch it march across the plasma that covers one wall of the office. I have parameters set up to catch the potential of the movement, or to let it flow according to my interests. Calls come in on seventeen telephones, and some of them I answer. In my baskets the cell phones ring incessantly. Various configurations and graphs display—pie charts, flow charts, bar charts, elliptical projections, the calculus of need, the topology of the apparent, fisting into the irrational. I've got open pockets for the virus. That's moolah, Do-Re-Mi; that's bucks. Wisdom is not to grab too much. Too much can be fatal. Just enough is a state of equilibrium. I set a goal—twice the mortgage and maintenance payment on my loft each day. Elegant is when I arrive at that amount at my first yawn, at the moment I am about to pack it in. Sometimes I don't quite get there, or am ready to leave when the day is in the red. That's expected. For the last ten years, at least, the monthly balance has always been in my favor. Even when the dot-com bubble burst, the virus and myself remained compatible. Goodbye art, hello money hello death.

As often happens, on certain days when everything seems to slide right into place, I reach my quota early, and am ready to leave long before the work day ends. I'm just putting my pencils back into their trays, so to speak, and about to straighten my lapels one last time, when Hilda buzzes my phone, tells me the president has arrived. Some of his Secret Service brutes are cute, she tells me. I had almost forgotten about this meeting, and am relieved that I don't have to plan a trip to Texas or D.C.

"Make them comfortable in the conference room," I tell her, "and I'll be there in just a moment."

It's flattering that in this time of war, economic turmoil, protests on the street, the president can spare a few moments for our meeting. I watch him through the glass wall of the conference room, drinking Cherry Coke from a can. He is a cute president. He circumambulates the table. One of his people empties the Cherry Coke into a paper cup, and he carries that with him. We must love him for his John Wayne swaggerette, as he strains to make us think he's a real Texas cowboy and not the mediocre Yale punk we know him for. It's hard to make out just where the evil resides. He has help, of course, from the vice one, Cheney, smirking over his various oil fortunes, busy making more; and the Goebbels of the bunch, Rumsfeld, small and self-important; and John Ashcroft, the poor, bloated fundamentalist.

Hilda winks at me as I go by. She sits on the lap of one of the Secret Service men, reading to him some good passages from *Jude The Obscure*. I submit to the frisking before I enter the room. One of the brutes calls another over to feel the fabric of my double-breasted jacket. Weighted silk. They slap me on the butt, and I enter the room with the president. He actually stands up again to shake my hand, and before our meeting begins, asks if I want a Cherry Coke. He tells me how much he favors Cherry Coke, now that he no longer takes a drink. Nothing cherry, I say, and we both laugh before getting down to serious business.

I step off the elevator, into what is usually the comfort and solace of my own space, but this evening I feel something different. For one thing, Ilyana's coat is still on the rack. She almost always leaves on Monday mornings, to spend a few days at her own apartment, often 'til the next weekend. I call her name, get no response. Andrew is not on his perch, hasn't even nibbled on the loquats I placed in his cage, isn't playing hide-and-seek with me in one of his usual hideaways. I hear some rustling in the bedroom, which is an enclosed platform, cantilevered off one bearing wall, reached by a curved stairway. I listen at the foot of those stairs to the bedclothes whipping around up there.

I remove my suede Vans, and tiptoe up the stairs, pausing on each step to listen for what I fear is going on in the darkened bedroom. Carefully, carefully I move. I pick up a jar of Dilly Beans someone opened and carried halfway up to the bedroom. There comes an ecstatic grunt, then an unmistakable cry of pleasure. This is not good. At last I stand in the doorway of my bedroom, and when my eyes adjust to the darkness I find my worst fears are realized. That vile parrot is in bed with Ilyana. A jar of pickled okra sits open on the nightstand. I put down the Dilly Beans.

Andrew is of the African Grey species, his accursed breed famous for its infinite capacity for mimicry.

The wretched bird peeks out from under the covers, and rips at the comforter with his beak. Goosedown erupts into the air that had been so corrupted this morning by crackers. Ilyana opens her eyes, sees me, and sits up suddenly, pulling my sheets over her breasts.

"It's not what you think," she says.

"I never thought I could do it, Andrew, but when there's a challenge I face up to it. That's my M.O. I was perched, you know, because as a parrot I do perch, and I was saying to myself, *Andrew, you good for nothing parrot guy, what the hell are you doing with your life. Maybe it's the time to lay something on the line. Maybe it's time to do your own thing.* So I went for it, just like that. And you know what? I can do it. Yeah. I'm up to it. I'm a goddamned helicopter of free love, Andrew."

The fucking parrot says he's a fucking helicopter.

Ilyana cowers, as if she would have me believe she is

afraid of what I might do. Each time she moves, more goose-down squirts into the air. What can I do? Kofi Annan mildly, diplomatically scolds us for our war. Putin pontificates. Little bitty Rumsfeld claims the Iraqis aren't fighting fair. Mike Tyson tattoos his face. Everything we do turns Saddam the Beast into Saddam the Martyr. Ry Cooder has been prohibited from returning to Cuba to get the music. China strengthens out of bounds. Which way Albania? Do we fight to make Iraq safe for bin Laden? My mind is excited but my heart is tired. Do I love her any less for finding her in bed with my bird?

"It's still not what you think," she repeats.

"Not what you think, *grawk*."

"Then what is it?"

"A dance piece I'm working on, to go with those poems."

"What dance piece? What is it about?" I recoil from the sarcasm in my own voice. "How to avoid AIDS by sleeping with anything from the order of Psittaciformes?"

"AIDS, *grawk*! Auto Immune Deficiency Syndrome, *grawk*!"

"You're not listening to me. This is one of the movements from the piece. I will perform it with Andrew at the Alternative Space, or at the Alternative Alternative Space. I have only a month to rehearse. You walked in on a rehearsal. You could have knocked."

"Rehearsal. Rehearsal?" The parrot swoops at Ilyana in the bed. "I'm a fucking helicopter, *grawk*."

"Andrew, please don't think I was...not with your Andrew," Ilyana pleads. She whips her hands from under the covers, and lifts them as if in prayer, both hands aglow. The air around her is bright with goosedown. It's a snow scene sealed in a globe. It's love thwarted by dandruff.

"What were the pickles for?" I whisper into nowhere, as I turn back down the stairs.

I take to my half-lotus position on my meditation cushion.

I sit.

Who am I to intervene? I love them both. I bless them both.

I sit.

Andrew circles my head, coming down in a tight spiral, and paces back and forth in front of me as if weighing some issues. Finally he stops to look at me.

"Andrew," says he. "So did you talk to the president?"

"I talked to him, Andrew."

"Did you mention the plight of the parrot, particularly the African Grey?"

"I asked him whether he thought that in order to defeat the beast, we had to become the beast?"

"Did he say African Grey?"

"He said, 'What are you talking about? God is on our side, and our weapons have pinpoint accuracy.'"

"And the parrot, Andrew? How about it?"

"I asked him how he and his posse could sleep at night, having gone to war on a gamble, and having put so many peoples' lives in jeopardy, both American and otherwise. Did they ever have second thoughts?" I asked.

"And what did he say about the African Grey?"

"He said our weapons are precise, and God is on our side. So I asked him when he spoke to God, did he ever run into the pope, who says God is not on our side in this war. Perhaps he talked with him on a conference call with the Almighty?"

"Did he say anything about the parrot's dilemma?"

"I asked him what he would do if bin Laden were near a hospital, a school, an orphanage, a middle class neighborhood, a slum, a marketplace, a concert, a hammam, a coffeehouse. Would he fire his missile?"

"What did he say, Andrew?"

"He said God was with us, on our side, and our weapons have pinpoint."

Andrew beat his wings. I pitied Andrew, his problems so specific. "I asked him how long he figured the War would take, and he told me to stop asking stupid questions. I told him that anyone who has a loved one in the war, or anyone who has feelings for humanity, wants some kind of reassurance, some kind of handle on the thing. It's not a stupid question. He says it will take as long as it takes, and to stop whining."

"Was he willing to talk about parrots?"

"I told him we weren't some children in the back of a car complaining to know when we would get there. I told him he should put on a uniform himself, put one on Condoleeza, put one on Ari Fleischer, on the young Rumsfelds and Cheneys. Can Ashcroft have kids? Put them out there in the sandstorms."

"About the African Grey, what did he say?"

"I asked what if they found bin Laden, and Osama was in bed with his wife, with Laura? Would he fire his weapon then?"

"*Grawk.*" Andrew lifted himself off floor, dropping some tail feathers as he flew to his perch. Grey feathers, fringed with black.

"He said he trusted his wife, the weapons were precise, could penetrate a bunker through a small hole. And God was on his side."

I sit. And I know that throughout the city, and throughout many cities in this time zone and later in the other time zones, many people will have settled onto their cushions, and are and will be sitting with me. Let us all sit. Sit 'til we fit.

The noise of the street barely reaches my cushion, hardly makes it through the insulation. A fan circulates warm air down. Many people freeze in the night on the streets. I am not yet them. I visualize the countryside, the beauty of it. I see a waterfall. I see long blond beaches with perfect waves. I look into my thoughts and see off the side of a mountain that wears a necklace of small sapphire lakes. This is refreshing. This gives a sense of well-being. From somewhere, as if a solitary bee were grazing in and out of earshot through the blossoming clover, a sound of war buzzes, gleaned from TVs in my building, and radios, and pulled down from satellites.

I sit, despite all, I sit.

A muffled scream from out there. An argument. Thoughts. Send them away. That could have been a gunshot? Yeah. I have, I know, an illusion of separation from the misery out there by this thin green veil of money. This is money I have earned. We have seen how volatile the green veil is. How quickly we can be exposed, and onto the street. A moment of conflagration, and it's gone, all security. I live here in a world of bubble wrap and Styrofoam peanuts. Andrew lives with me. Ilyana is here sometimes. Outside of where I live the life blisters, the life of others. Inside, the pressures are slight, and have little significance. But what is outside, and what is inside all is taken into the heart, weighed and measured there, and it does weigh, and that is what is meant when the heart is heavy.

"The heart is heavy. The heart is heavy. *Grawk.*"

NOWADAYS & HEREAFTER

THE TRUE ANIMATED FABLE

I

No sandart any more, no sandbook, no masters

—*Paul Celan*

He escaped, chasing after his shadow, broken from his losses. The mango tree that had once protected him was ripped from the earth, its pale rootlets drying in the sun. Tignee had twined his legs into the branches trying to hold onto his wife, but the flood-tide was brutal. It tore her from his hands, and then baby floated out of her arms and away, like a bubble. His son too lost his grip, sank and rose and sank again 'til he was out of sight. One of his wife's sandals had snagged in the roots, the blue stones that decorated its straps still shining. He buckled its strap to his wrist.

The ones returning now to the nowhere paradise he was leaving dragged their shadows behind them.

He tried to speak with one or another, but no one responded, as if those who had once been his neighbors were too numbed now to recognize someone they had lived with all their lives. As they returned to the sea they passed through what remained of this impoverished empire of stuff, some of it small as threads, some as large as the wrecks of fishing boats. They gathered the shards and flecks of the former shrines in order, he guessed, to make an offering when they took themselves back to the water's edge.

He was leaving a place he thought he remembered, but perhaps he remembered incorrectly. The pain he felt was correct, somehow. Perhaps he was a tourist. Did he come from there, a place now erased? Was he moving in the right direction away from or towards a somewhere? He didn't want to look behind. Had he ever lived in the nowhere he was leaving? The questions were sad jokes. Perhaps he had been a tourist, just a tourist in a paradise that has been erased. Village, gone. Family, gone. He lifted his hands to examine scars and calluses from spinning fiber and knotting nets. He had been an architect of the nets. That memory was incised on his palms.

In the midst of the stragglers coming towards him he spotted a boy, handsome and slim as his son. He looked to be eight or nine, the age of his own boy. Perhaps he had escaped or had been rescued from the tide. He wasn't sure this was Ekey, not absolutely sure. Perhaps his vision was fading. That he couldn't with certainty distinguish his son from the flow of young people returning troubled him. Nonetheless, as the boy approached he readied himself to greet him. The boy had seemed to spot Tignee from afar, and seemed to be happily rushing towards him. As he drew closer Tignee still wasn't sure, absolutely sure, this was his son. A man should know his own son, he scolded himself. He should easily distinguish him from anyone else. They approached, and were within reach of each other as Tignee held out his arms. Without a glance, without a smile or a high five, the boy passed him by. He totally ignored the man who might have been his father. Now Tignee faced the quandary of whether or not to turn back and grab the boy. Or should he keep going, assume he had been mistaken? Youth would go its own way, had to have its own destiny. He soon had to accept that there was no way out of his quandary, no way to answer his questions, so he continued walking into the shadows. His own shadow shortened in front of him, as if it was his to consume. The light pinked into evening as he went. The bulbuls and flowerpeckers and babblers sang into the retreating light, bright shadows jumping branch to branch. He had been only a tourist, he decided, like all the tourists, only a visitor, a spinner and weaver of nets in this deleted paradise. Anyone could be no more than a visitor in paradise.

He spent the night by the side of the road, and in the early morning started to climb into the hills. The road rose slowly at first, then steepened through the plantations of coffee trees. The red berries glowed in the evenly planted rows like tiny lamps at a celebration. He picked some berries and bit them. They were sweet, very unlike the taste of coffee. He could not account for his good cheer, considering what he thought he remembered from the past week. He tallied his losses. Tignee lost his wife. Tignee lost his baby. Everything connected with his livelihood, Tignee lost. Tignee lost his house. Tignee lost his boy. Tignee lost his business. Tignee lost all his whalebone netting needles. Tignee lost his spindles. Tignee lost a recently sharpened set of scissors. Tignee lost his village. Tignee lost his nets. Tignee lost the box of jewelry his wife had asked him to keep for her: a gold ring, a ruby bracelet. Tignee lost his three-wheel truck. Tignee lost his mother, and her friends. Tignee lost his knives. As much as he kept adding losses, nothing could defeat his sense of well-being, the feeling that everything was in order, all for the best, everything had a purpose. How could that be? His calm was unshakable and disturbing. This was a nasty way to feel about what had happened. He began to suspect that perhaps he wasn't this Tignee of his thoughts, but a different person who witnessed this catastrophe. But if he wasn't Tignee, from where did he get his thoughts of Tignee? And who could he be otherwise?

Beyond the shallow slopes of coffee trees, the jungle stretched upwards towards the clouds. Palm fronds and broad leaves covered the road. They slipped under his feet, making him stumble. Occasionally he stepped through a smoky breeze that smelled almost human. Sounds, at first dim but slowly getting louder, reached him as the road rose into the clouds. They were inviting him upwards, beckoning him into obscurity. An occasional scooter or truck passed, leaving an acrid perfume of exhaust, refreshing. Sounds of birds and monkeys filled the dense jungle. They said *peeweep peeweep sweet sweet some sweet mapa pama*. As he ascended the sounds articulated more into words, phrases too complicated for the birds—*Jasmine eats the bugs; bake the butter cookies six potato seven potato eleven potato*. He slowly penetrated the layer of clouds and rose to a broad plateau of trees. What he saw there among the trees made him wonder. Children lived there in the limbs. In each of the live oaks, among the branches, and in the flowering jacarandas, and in the wild cocoa, and the gumbo limbo, clambering from limb to limb, a human child lived its monkey-life. Below each tree, the adults, the parents, or what he took to be the parents, beseeched the children to come down. "That's enough now of your shenanigans." "Come down, no more monkeyshines." "We're going to leave without you. We're not fooling." "Okay, come down now. We're ready to go!" "This is your last chance. Bye bye."

Where would they go, he wondered? Where was there to go, he wanted to know?

Their entreaties, perfunctory and hopeless, flitted up through the dark leaves like moths, into the blue, cloudless sky. He wandered among the families, if that's what they were, listening to each of them entreat their children. It was a wide plateau of trees—lychee and bottlebrush, mahogany and sprawled weeping figs. Under almost every tree a small fire burned as the families prepared to cook. From high in the branches of a trumpet tree a dark-eyed boy stared and blinked and stared some more, long enough for him to think it might be his son. What was the name? He approached the tree. "Ekey," he called, as he remembered. "Maniwan," called someone approaching from the other side of the tree. Maniwan was not the name of his son. The woman spoke a language he didn't recognize. "Maniwan," she called, waving him down from his perch with a bandaged hand. The boy ignored her, and looked away from Tignee. A man carrying a baby followed. She lowered one side of her smock, cradled the baby with her wrapped hand, and took the child to her breast. The child burrowed into her breast with a loud suck. Down to the reddish curl that spiraled from above the brow, the baby looked exactly like the infant he lost when his wife plunged. He wondered if the woman had injured her hand. The husband filled a bucket that the boy in the tree had lowered on a rope with some flatbread cooked in a pan on their small fire, a bowl of soup, and an earthen jug of water.

He approached the couple, and spoke, "Hello." The man rose from where he had been kneeling by the fire, and bowed to Tignee, who bowed back, though it wasn't his custom.

Tignee put his palm to his chest, which was his custom. "My name is Tignee. I come from..." He pointed towards the sea. He was reluctant to speak the name of his obliterated village.

The man lifted a pan off the fire and offered Tignee a wedge of the flatbread. "Kemekme," the man said. Tignee didn't know if that was his name or the word in his language for the bread he was offering.

The bread, crisp and slightly sweet, crumbled in his mouth. "What is this place? Why is everyone here?" he asked, looking from the man to the nursing woman. Neither answered him. "When did everyone come here?" They didn't understand his language, he guessed. They seemed friendly enough to answer out of courtesy, but they gave no response. Tignee looked away. Throughout the forest small fires bloomed as if it was a happy season.

The baby sucked hard because it wanted to be alive. Sweat beaded its forehead. The mother changed supporting hands to wipe the child's brow with her bandage. The babe backed off the breast from time to time and threw its head back, milk trapped in the creases of its pucker, to stare up at the brother who gazed on it from his treelimb.

"Do you think the baby will join its brother in the tree?" Tignee asked, not expecting an answer.

The father squatted between the tree and the fire, sharpening a set of chisels. He gathered some small saws, small knives of various shapes, miters, calipers, all tools of the joiner's trade. He rolled these implements carefully in leather, and placed them in a pack, and when he was done he slung this across one shoulder. He kissed his wife, and the baby, saluted the boy in the tree, and set off in the direction opposite to what Tignee would have expected, were he going to lend his skills where Tignee knew they were needed, to help rebuild by the shore.

The mother put the child down after it stopped nursing, and watched it crawl along a tree root. She smiled at Tignee as her baby, moving like a lizard, started up the tree trunk to be with its brother. Tignee bowed to the woman, and turned to wander among the others in this vast encampment.

A long file of men walked in twos and threes, carrying the tools of their various skills, headed in the direction that Tignee had been taking as he fled catastrophe. They were fleeing nothing. Where were they headed? It was early evening, and the sun was setting in the direction they were going. How long would they walk? How far would they go?

He turned away to wander off in the twilight through the woods from one small fire to the next. He whispered the name of Ekey, speaking it to himself, repeating Ekey over and over, until it became pure sound, void of significance. That sound was absorbed into the hum of the wind pumps, which the people had built here and there among the trees to pump water from shallow wells. Along a strip of rocks that bisected the plateau people filled bladders and bags with a gas that escaped from small vents. It smelled like iodine and hyacinth, and was lighter than air, so that using these bladders as balloons, they could float provisions to the small ones in the trees.

"Mr. Sir. Please. Over here." The voice of a young woman beckoned him. "Sir. Over here. Please."

A young woman sat by a glow of embers beneath a mahogany tree. She held out a bowl and gestured with her chin for him to sit down beside her.

"Cassava and greens," she said as he took the bowl. She

wasn't, he thought, more than sixteen years old. She handed him a spoon, and touched the sandal Tignee had forgotten was buckled to his wrist. A whistle from above made Tignee look up.

"My brother," she said, and she removed the sandal from his wrist and placed it on the ground. Without straightening from her squat she shuffled to a small stash of possessions that was hidden under some leaves, and pulled out an object wrapped carefully in newspaper.

"This is that," she said, and placed it next to the sandal.

The food she had given him was delicious, the cassava hearty, the slight bitterness of the greens balanced by pea-sized cubes of fragrant meat. He thanked her, and they sat for a few moments staring at the package and the sandal.

"My name is Sylva," she finally said, and took his hand in both hers.

The warmth of her hands and her gentle dark eyes reassured Tignee, and restored him to himself enough so he could say, "My name is Tignee. I am a weaver of nets. I repaired nets by the sea." A dull swell of pride crept up. "I taught myself to spin a whole new fiber for my nets, like threads stronger than steel. And I invented a knot that allows it to stretch, but never to break." He extracted a small square of netting from his pocket, and handed it to her. She wrapped her fingers through it, and stretched. The netting disintegrated, as if it had been baked and only ash was left. He remembered now that this wasn't his netting, famous new and unconquerable, but it was a random piece of old netting that had been caught in the mango tree, that he had taken, just to have something.

"That is not the net. Not mine," he explained, and as if the faucet had suddenly opened he started to tell her all that had happened. Everything had disappeared—his wife, his children, his business, all his miserable story.

"The water suddenly rose, without warning, to drown away the whole world. I always thought the ocean had been my friend, gave nourishment to my village. We lived from the gifts of papa ocean. But now I realize that was nothing but a foolish enchantment. The waters are indifferent, and can as easily slaughter as sustain. Ocean has no intention and no regrets."

The compassion in her look was far more mature than what he took to be her sixteen years. Her youthful beauty had been deepened, toughened, as it was annealed in the fires of loss and despair.

"I was hoping," he said softly, afraid to say it aloud, "that if I came in this direction, by luck or by chance I would find my wife, my older son here, somewhere. My baby. They were all torn away from me." He had never expressed this hope before, not even to himself.

Sylva lifted two skewers off the embers, each of which pierced three small birds. Their skin was crisp, their wingtips charred. She handed one skewer to Tignee.

"My brother catches these." Tignee looked up at the tree limb. The brother watched them, without making a sound. "Our father was a gamekeeper and with our mother, brother and sisters, we lived in a bird sanctuary on the outskirts of the great city of Avnikra, where we were all happy. Tewly learned these skills from father, so he knows how to invite small birds into our pot. Our father was a gentle man."

The birds, stuffed with nuts and raisins, filled his mouth with flavor. He raised the skewer to the brother in the tree, to thank him. The boy was already asleep. Sylva placed some chips of bark on the embers, so fire flared up. She and Tignee watched the flames.

"What became of your father, your mother? Where are your other brothers, your sister?" Tignee asked, afraid of what he might hear.

"My father adjured me to take my little brother here to these woods, where children lived in the trees, like the birds and the monkeys."

The description of her father pierced Tignee's heart, as if it was an arrow aimed flat into whatever else he might have done as a father. "Where is he now? Why did he send you two here alone?"

"He knew they would take him. There was nothing he could do, one man opposing all the power of hatred and war. You look at the situation and nothing makes sense. Nothing ever recovers the price of war. Nothing undoes its misery. He was one man against the surge of violence, a tide of blindness."

"Who are they? Why your father?"

"They are who they are. Some of them live in here," she pressed a hand into Tignee's chest. He shook his head to negate.

"He is a strong and capable man with many skills, as are my older brothers. My mother he told to escape to the sea, with baby Viska."

The thought of escaping to the sea made Tignee shiver. Sylva took his hand. Together they listened to the wind. The fire warmed their faces. Sylva's tears dried into streaks. "War, my father told me, is a dragon with many heads that devours everyone, everything around it. He knew we would be safe here; at least, he thought so. One of my older brothers ran away, towards the sea, and my mother followed with the baby."

"When was this?"

"It was a month ago, I think. Some day soon Tewly and I will go to the sea to find them."

Tignee let out a cry. Could it be that she didn't understand what had happened? "Which way did your father go?"

She pointed in the direction he had seen the men march off earlier with their tools. Tignee tried not to weep. She touched his shoulder. "Don't worry. I expect my father to come back, though I don't think he will ever again be the gentle man-of-the-birds."

They both looked down again, back to the sandal, and the package next to it. With the tip of her foot, she pushed it towards Tignee. He looked at her in a confusion of thoughts. Who was she? She was very young, yet he had these feelings for her. She gestured for him to pick up the package. He looked through the deepening darkness into the reflections of the small fires in her eyes. He slowly removed the newspaper, an advertisement for cosmetics, free giveaway with every purchase. What it had wrapped was the other sandal, a mate to the one he had been carrying. He turned away from it as if it was a light that blinded him.

Sylva steadied Tignee as he was about to stagger backwards. He dropped the wrapper into the fire and it flew up, a wing of flame burning past the brother asleep in the tree. "You know what it is, yes?"

He was sure it was the other sandal, his Marti's other sandal. He knew the imprint of his wife's small foot in the footbed. The blue stones glistened like eyes. He stared at the pair for a long time, numb to his own confusion and feelings. He thought he could see his wife step into them and run away into the forest. "Marti," he called. The children in their sleep let out brittle cries as she disappeared, their voices like glass bells struck in the trees.

"I was, I think, waiting for you to come with this other one. I thought and thought about it, how I wanted to wear them. I wondered where the mate could be."

He picked the sandal up and held it in front of her face. "How did you get this?"

"Do you think I could...?"

"Where did it come from?" he insisted. "I want to know, did she...?"

"I would like very much to wear them," she said.

Tignee threw the sandal to the ground. "Then wear them."

Sylva slipped her feet into the sandals, and stood before him as if she was his wife. She smiled at him. This smile was too familiar, and it made him feel ill at ease in his confusion and anger. In a few moments she left the ground and rose like the paper he had burned, to her brother's place in the tree. She smoothed his hair, and kissed him. As Tignee watched her circle, in the darkness above the tree, seven times around the fire, he knew that all this life was a charade, and that he had come to rest in a forest of ghosts.

II

I hear they call life
The only shelter

—Paul Celan

After several weeks of waking up with Sylva next to him Tignee finally began to feel comfortable, as if this was where he was supposed to be. The loss of his family had numbed his heart, and attention to the lot of these two revived it again. He continued to hope that if he remained in these woods perhaps his wife and children would show up, or at least someone with news of their fate. When he lay down with Sylva that first night it was in innocence. He feared her youth and respected her purity. He was determined not to touch her. He sat up once that night, startled at a sound. She pressed him back down.

"Don't worry. It's just the panthers that wander by."

"Panthers?"

"You can't see them. During the day they sleep, and they come through at night."

He didn't understand why, but the word "panther" and the idea of its invisibility, rattled Tignee. He felt a surge of desire. "Panther" struck some erotic channel, and he grew hard. When she felt his cock poke her thigh Sylva stirred herself and sucked him into a warm pocket in her body. At that point her youth became an irrelevant cipher.

The physicality, if he could call it that, soon became strange and marvelous. Each night, as they lay down, he felt the weight, the warmth, the very pores of her skin against his, at first all very comforting. As he drifted into his own fantasies before sleep, she became increasingly less substantial beside him. In the mornings, when he was awakened each day by the mischief of Tewly, who dropped bits of bark down, to remind them to start a fire for breakfast, he would reach across to touch Sylva and find nothing palpable. But as he brought more of an image of her to mind she would materialize slowly next to him, forming like a galaxy being nudged into shape by dark matter, until he could finally sense her as on their first encounter. He felt that to get to her it was as if he had to push through a cloud of gnats to come up against a tree, or as if her flesh alone was shy and could hide away until it was persuaded into substance. For him it was a source of exhilaration.

So Tignee stayed and as he wandered among the families of shades in the encampment, watched them feed and wash, make music and dance as if they were alive, he began to notice that the irregularity underfoot wasn't caused just by tree roots close to the surface. As he brushed the soil aside with his sandal in places where it was thin he recognized that he was treading on bone. Human bone formed the substrate of this plateau. So many, he marveled, had died to create this elevation of specters. It stretched as far as he could see in every direction. He suspected that the whole plateau, from sea level to where he was standing, rose up as a heap of bones.

"Is there anyone who hasn't died?" he asked, throwing his head back as if the answer might be in the sky.

"Life is the most temporary accident," Sylva said.

"Have at it," said her brother, hanging upside down from a limb of his tree.

At night he lay beside the dim essence of Sylva and waited for a deeper darkness, but none ever came. The bone glowed everywhere beneath the duff and debris, and where bone was exposed it cast a spectral radiance. Sometimes Tignee got up and walked about feeling the glow around him, a shine that seemed to make him light, as if he were on the surface of the moon.

As he circulated among the shades of people at rest, and felt the thrill of panthers sliding through the dim shadows, he soon started to realize what he would have to do. This became so happily obvious, he went about with a broad grin for several days before he started to do anything.

"What?" asked Sylva, giggling herself, as Tignee's good mood was infectious.

"You'll see," he said.

He collected the cleanest, strongest, most flexible bones he could uncover. Sylva watched him in the evening, as he rubbed them together to harden them, and began to scrape them with stone, to whittle them down. She watched him carve the bone into shapes he seemed to know very well.

"This is the spindle to spin the twine," he showed it to Sylva and to her brother in the tree. "And this is the needle to braid the nets. We make needles in several sizes, according to the gauge of the net, and we measure that with this mesh gauge."

Sylva and Tewly gathered some bones for themselves, and started to fashion the implements under Tignee's tutelage. As they worked, others arrived from other encampments and fires, to learn how to fashion these tools. Soon there was a good supply, and Tignee knew that the time was right to start to spin the fiber.

This fiber, as he conceived it, was spun of threads shed from a yuccalike plant, that had to be soaked in the urine of the marmot. To collect enough of this urine was no small trick, but when he explained it to the spectral population of this plateau, they wasted no time taking advantage of the fact that marmots have no fear of human ghosts. The other element in his fiber is made from the leaf of the Yonoletenus bush, which grows near the shore as a tree, to a height of forty-three feet or more, but at this altitude manifests as a bush no higher than six feet. You could create a fiber of the mature leaves of this plant by chewing them thoroughly, enduring the bitterness and dryness of palate that results, and extruding the product through the smallest pucker you could form. This product crystallizes into a fiber that when spun together with the fibers of the succulent creates a thread that will never fatigue. Although Tignee knew of it, a little-recognized fact of nature is that the saliva of the ghost is a powerful fortifying agent. When the Yonoletenus fibers are chewed down with ghost spittle, the resulting cord is undefeatable.

Tignee circulated among the shades, teaching them spinning techniques, how to make twine of different thicknesses, and increase the elasticity, until he had substantial amounts of a variety of twines rolled into easily accessible balls. Then he moved further among the ghosts to teach them how to braid nets, to use different needles for different gauges, how to apply the mesh gauges and keep it uniform. After a while he saw that over the whole plateau vast expanses of net covered the encampment of shades and their ghostly progeny in the trees. For Tignee this was a beautiful sight. The nets were tougher than steel, and though the sweet shades that produced them could pass through easily, nothing of substance would ever defeat it. Though he didn't know yet what the use would be for all the netting his instruction had produced, he knew that eventually it would all be necessary.

One evening, as Tignee lay awake in the persistent twilight of the plateau of ghosts he became aware of some noise, a dim and distant clamor in the auditory substrate, barely audible, a metallic clanging and scraping, unlike the clear resonance of the bells that once rang in his village.

When Sylva rose the next day, he asked her if she heard it.

"I hear it all the time," she said.

"Do you know what it is?"

"I do," she said, and looked up to Tewly on his branch, spreading her arms as if she wanted to embrace him.

"Then what is it?" Tignee asked.

Sylva pointed in the direction her father had gone, the direction in which all the men had marched off. "Ay, Pancho. Ahime," she exclaimed, and for only the second time she put on Marti's sandals and rose through the branches to be with her brother, and they gathered the netting around themselves and disguised themselves within it, as if they had been caught.

Tignee rested among the shades on their plateau for one hundred and thirty-six weeks, during which time he learned a great deal, and passed on as much as he could of his own special knowledge. He was gratified to see how quickly they had produced many square miles of net, all of it of great strength. At the beginning of the one hundred and thirty-seventh week he found himself folding a square of fine mesh around some food and a few belongings. He was preparing to leave. It was a surprise to himself because he hadn't expected to leave, nor had he told Sylva and Tewly he would ever go away.

"Why?" she asked. "Where can you go?"

Tignee pointed in the direction of the grinding noise that was only slightly audible when you listened hard, as the sound of an orchestra sometimes leaks incoherently into the street through the cracks of a great music hall. It surprised Tignee that Sylva wept, and when Tignee touched her tears to wipe them away he learned that the tears of such a specter are colder than ice, and brought blisters to his fingertips.

"Will you come back?" she asked. Tignee shrugged, because he couldn't even explain why he was leaving.

"Have at it," said the brother from the tree.

"Have at what?" Tignee asked the boy.

Tewly was swinging by one arm, like a monkey ghost. "Then have at it again."

"And again," he shouted at Tignee's back, when at the start of his one hundred and thirty-seventh week, Tignee set out to continue in the direction he had been going, in the direction he had seen most of the men march away. He turned back to wave at the shades that had been his companions, and they let out in unison a spectral moan that was like a wind at his back. Once he got to the place where the road suddenly steepened, he turned back a second time and saw nothing but an expanse of devastation, no trees left, burnt to charred stumps. Wind gusts sucked swirls of ash into the air.

He followed the sharp rise of road away. A stream of icy water flowed down the center. He had never experienced cold like this before. He had never seen snow before. His whole body trembled as he walked. The wind left heaps of the cold white powder in his way, so he had to step through it, his feet protected only by some light socks inside thin sandals. From time to time he had to stop to rub his feet and bring them back to life. He heard clearly now in the cold air the grind of big machines in motion. They played out so crisply he could hear the tone and rasp of each wheel and each gear.

Before dark, he gathered some brush and dried lichen and made a small fire by striking sparks from some flinty rocks. He roasted a small yam he had brought, and ate it with some scraps of dried meat. The walking, all of it up a steep mountainside, had made him bone-tired but he imagined the cold would keep him awake through the night. He twisted on the sharp grass, brown and cold on his back. Then he saw Orion's belt, bright as daggers. Each of the sisters of the Pleiades pulsed with such power that he felt them shield him from the cold, and under those stars he was able to fall asleep.

On the next morning he woke frozen into the fog as if inside a block of ice. He breathed in short gulps. The air was acrid with exhaust and the stench of human waste. Tignee stepped as if blinded onto the road that descended into a valley solid with the clank of machines. He could hardly see in front of himself, and moved trusting only what his feet could feel on the other side of the mountain—one foot, then the other foot into the gloom. He was a man, he realized, who had no power even to guess at what might happen to him next. He had given up the possibility that somewhere along this route he would encounter Marti and his kids, or even someone who knew of them. This was a different life from that life he had once been living—this was a life of moving blindly, his other a life of keeping a still watch.

The sun with deft hands folded the fog away like white sheets off a line. Once he passed between two great curved granite cliffs that leaned almost into a tunnel above him he could see what stretched below: an expanse of valley, a vast plain he had only heard about, and never seen before. As the clouds passed below him over the land, he saw masses of men and machines that from these heights seemed to be pushed into order from place to place by an invisible broom. The clamor reached him with the upslope winds, sometimes loud, sometimes softer, always machines clanking and roaring, but also an undercurrent of mumbling, familiar mumbling, incessant mumbling. People, perhaps. What stories might they be telling? The tanks, the armored personnel vehicles, the Hummers, the great cannons on half-tracks, the trucks hauling ammunition and provisions, the missile launchers, the reinforced dozers and excavators, all maneuvered as a mass, an integrated juggernaut assembled to destroy. What were the words, Tignee wondered, that so mumbled or pronounced could manufacture and move this juggernaut? Tignee rested and watched through the rest of the afternoon, slept that night under the lip of a cliff that had been warmed by the sun. In the morning, when sanguine threads of dawn stitched across the horizon, he rose into the new day, washed his face with some water dripping from the cliff, and descended further to where the noise and movement originated.

If what he had been through hadn't already annulled all his hope, what he saw here might have startled him into paralysis and silence. He wandered through fields of everyone, some kneeling as if in prayer, before a wide array of crucifixes, a figure nailed to each, those figures made of straw, and the mumbling worshippers, straw men as well. Others with foreheads to the ground mumbled beneath a star and sickle moon, flesh translucent and wobbling as if they were adrift in the sea. And so many more were dressed in black, and swayed before six-pointed stars that crumbled with them as they collapsed into heaps of cinder. Many licked a sugar-boodle Buddha that shrank away from their tongues, as the tongues got longer and intertwined. Tignee had never seen so much humanity constrained and bounded by concept and illusion. Many of them were maimed, had lost limbs, had wide suppurating gashes in head and thorax and back. Their wounds leaked blood and pus. There were children dying in their mothers' arms, and mothers dying with sucklers at their breasts. Still this throng mumbled conflicting entreaties to their exclusive systems of grace, as if they were protecting the endless spread of missiles that rose everywhere around them dense as corn on a prairie. Above all this, flocks of helicopters and fighter planes and bombers and drones turned and swooped in and out of sight like masses of starlings.

Throughout the ranks of men and women moved every chimera that the sun sucks up. The lion's head roared the decrees into the mob, while from its tail, a serpent hissed a litany of penalties, and from its back the head of a goat bleated in an exaltation of pain. They demanded obedience. Creatures from mythologies yet to be written deployed among the humans, whipping them into closer order. There were the obvious unicorns, the dragons, the centaurs, the gryphons, the winged horses ridden low over the crowd by Minotaur, a legion of snakes cackling through hyena heads, hippos with the face of the chimpanzee, panda faces with the bodies of ocelots. There was a fox that burrowed like a mole, rose where it was needed to snap people into position. And moles with wings flew in squadrons to cover the crowd with their crap. Many of these creatures Tignee couldn't begin to describe for himself. They all circled through the people, restraining them, reducing them to even rows. Tignee moved in awe among these wonders and aberrations, at first, without being noticed. The novelty of it fascinated him, and terrified him at the same time. He wanted to see it all, and to hide from it all. He sat for a long time on a hill, his back against a rock, trembling in awe. Tignee was afraid, but unable to dim his fascination. He felt a powerful temptation to join the people at prayer, any persuasion would do. They now seemed made not of straw or jelly or cinder, but of flesh vulnerable as his own. They were engaged in simple worship and surrender.

He was ready to surrender.

Suddenly, as if the wind had changed its channel, dirt and pebbles rattled down on him. A grenade had exploded below his position. Then another exploded to the right of him, and another. He had been found out. The whole machinery of war and destruction ceased its drills and maneuvers and rotated to face him. They started towards him as one complex dilemma that had chosen Tignee as its enemy. The sound rose through the octaves, in a frenzy of decibels. He was frozen in place. If he knew what to say he would have shouted something to tell them he intended no harm, he was no threat to them, but could think of nothing that would convince them of anything once they had turned to him. In their economy, harm and threat was small change. For them this was practice. For him, it was a question of living or dying. For them death was like a dessert. The question of what there was left of his life, if he continued, squirreled into his mind, but begged an answer. He had to act. He sprang away and ran zigzag up the hillside through a maze of exploding shells and bullets, kicking dust. Shrapnel tore his clothes and scraped his skin. The impact of explosions whipped him against trees and rocks as if he was a flag turned loose in the wind. He escaped direct hits, however. Maybe it was luck. He could smell his own fear. In an outcropping of rocks he hid in some small caves. Pressed against the wall of a cavern, he listened to the movement of the tanks outside, and jackboots crunching volcanic rock. All this expense of energy for the elimination of himself, he thought. One small figure alone. He would have been flattered had they come to enlist his expertise as the architect of nets. It might have been inappropriate, and counter to his intuitions, he reflected, for him to be on the side of a force of war, but he knew how weak he was, and admitted he was hungry for recognition. It was during this assault, while he was pressed against the wall of the cave, that he came up with his plan. It wouldn't be a sure thing, but it would be the effort of one man to resist this human inhumane tide.

Clouds covered the moon that evening, and Tignee slipped away undetected. He avoided the road and climbed over the cliffs. He sank to his hips in the snow, plunged on over the summit, and when dawn came he was still moving. He heard the machines grinding slowly behind him, and a huge sound from those enlisted on the march, like the yowling of a cosmic dog. He dragged his shadow down through the plateau where he had stayed before. The surviving trees showed some foliage, and a few skeletons remained scattered here and there in the realm of ghosts. He remembered the location of the tree where Sylva had been. The tree was badly charred, but had managed a few new leaves. A skeletal figure stepped from behind the tree, and he shuddered. *What is life?* thought Tignee. The specter approached Tignee, bony arms outstretched as if it wanted to embrace him. The sandals with their blue stones undamaged allowed him to recognize her. Marti's sandals were still attached, hooked to Sylva's feet. The feet were reduced to little more than their small bones.

"I knew you would come back," rasped the voice, with no trace of the lilt that Tignee had once enjoyed in Sylva's voice. In his arms she felt like a bundle of twigs. She leaned back and looked at him through sunken eyes rimmed with yellow scabs. Lesions festered in the skin stretched across the bones of her face. When she puckered to kiss him a clear thick fluid oozed from the cracks in her lips. As she drew close he shuddered and resisted. He closed his eyes and battled the nausea, as he smelled her putrefying face. But they kissed and the kiss was shockingly sweet. His arms and shoulders relaxed at the taste that reminded him of his Marti's mouth. A squawk from above turned them both to look up at the small figure dangling from a blackened branch. It was a diminutive bag of bones.

"Tewly?"

"He wants to tell you something."

Tignee looked up to listen, but could hardly hear above the noise growing around him. He shrugged at Sylva, and she understood, and rose as she had done before, but with more effort, as if a weak collaborator was turning a crank to help her rise. There was so little left of the poor boy up there. Tignee recognized now what sounds he was hearing around himself from the charred forest. "He is happy to see you," Sylva said when she rattled back down. "'Have at it,' is what he wants to say to you."

They were embedded in the sound of babies crying, a crying that went brutally to the heart of Tignee, as it would to the heart of any man who has been a father, a father who has lost his children. Tignee felt the need to do something, but he also felt helpless to do anything. He could hear babies who cried because they were hungry, and babies who cried because they were weak. Some babies cried because they were hurting. There were those who cried because they had been abandoned, and those who cried because they were lost, or woke to strange people touching them. There were those who cried because something tasted bad, because something burned their tongues. Some cried because they were left to chill in their own feces. Some cried for lack of milk. Some because they were swollen. Some cried because they were so small, some because what they saw coming was too big. But the loudest of them, and most pitiful of cries, came from those who didn't know why they cried. They had no reason to cry. They cried for no reason at all. .

Tignee was now even more determined to do what he had to do. In the morning, he gathered around himself all the remnants of what had once been a thriving empire of ghosts. All of them had abandoned their hauntings of the flesh and what remained was the thinnest residue of skin clinging to some phantom bones. He didn't know if, collectively, they would have enough strength to do what he needed done. He stayed with them therefore for one hundred and thirty-six days, designing and laying out traps and snares made of the nets he had previously taught them to braid. From the line of rock that crossed the plateau and emitted a gas smelling of iodine and hyacinth, he filled bladders made from the intestines of panthers—visible now because they were recently dead—and using these lifts he floated his lightest nets from the tallest trees left, so they rose out of sight to spread as a trap for airborne armaments. And they spread the heaviest nets along the ground far and wide, square miles of net, attached to the snares he devised that would devour the heaviest of the vehicles, and entangle whole armies tumbled into a pouch where they had to submit. *This is ready,* Tignee thought. On the one hundred and thirty-seventh day, he looked out at what the remains of his specters had accomplished, and said, "This is good."

He looked to the road, towards where he had escaped the assault, and saw the black line of disaster that swelled and brimmed along the ridge. From there an uncomfortable silence rolled down like noxious gas.

Tignee stood up and raised his arms. "Have at it, you sons of bitches. Have at it now," he shouted, and his cohorts rattled in echo.

And then, on this one hundred and thirty-seventh day, Tignee turned. He picked up one of the sandals, buckled it to his wrist, and set out. Tignee returned to the sea.